I0601334

LINNEA'S ARRANGEMENT

DIVINITY HEALERS

MICHELLE M. PILLOW

MICHELLE M. PILLOW® - MICHELLEPILLOW.COM

Linnea's Arrangement (Divinity Healers) © Copyright 2013-2017, Michelle M. Pillow

Second Print Edition July 2018

First Print Edition September 2017

First Electronic Printing November 2013

Published by The Raven Books LLC

ISBN 978-1-62501-185-5

ALL RIGHTS RESERVED.

This book or any portion thereof may not be reproduced or used in any manner whatsoever without the express written permission of the publisher except for the use of brief quotations in a book review.

This novel is a work of fiction. Any and all characters, events, and places are of the author's imagination and should not be confused with fact. Any resemblance to persons, living or dead, or events or places is merely coincidence.

Michelle M. Pillow® is a registered trademark of The Raven Books LLC

ABOUT LINNEA'S ARRANGEMENT

DIVINITY HEALERS BOOK THREE

Alternate Reality Romance, Part of the Divinity Universe

Beautiful, highly intelligent Linnea Nel wants what most women want—a career, love, respect. But coming from a plane where order and all things anti-chaos reign, the untrackable, untraceable and highly rebellious Linnea is considered a threat—to her family, society and her world. When her numerous arrests for reading library books become a public embarrassment to her politically minded sister, Linnea is forced on a dignitary mission to an alternate reality.

There are only two classifications of people on plane 187: Doctors and Not Doctors (Sans). Dr. Sam

Swift is one of the highest ranking officials on the medical plane, answering only to the Medical Supreme. When the Medical Supreme becomes ill, it's up to him to find a cure. Nowhere in this equation is there room—or time—to fall in love. And then he meets the exquisitely frustrating Sans Linnea Nel.

In the midst of the worst outbreak 187's society has faced in decades, two people who never should have met fall in love. How can Linnea stay where she may be in danger? But how can Sam let the love of his life go?

ABOUT DIVINITY HEALERS
SERIES

In Asclepius there are only two classifications of people. Doctors and Not Doctors (Sans). They are the go-to plane for anything medical. In fact, they're so focused on health it's become a bit of an obsession. Plants are encased in glass to protect people from allergens. The air is pumped full of chemicals to keep it sterile.

This is a plane teeming with germ-a-phobes.

MICHELLE'S BESTSELLING
SERIES

QURILIXEN WORLD NOVELS

Dragon Lords Series

Barbarian Prince

Perfect Prince

Dark Prince

Warrior Prince

His Highness The Duke

The Stubborn Lord

The Reluctant Lord

The Impatient Lord

The Dragon's Queen

Lords of the Var® **Series**

The Savage King

The Playful Prince
The Bound Prince
The Rogue Prince
The Pirate Prince

Captured by a Dragon-Shifter Series
Determined Prince
Rebellious Prince
Stranded with the Cajun
Hunted by the Dragon
Mischievous Prince
Headstrong Prince

Space Lords Series
His Frost Maiden
His Fire Maiden
His Metal Maiden
His Earth Maiden
His Woodland Maiden

Qurilixen Lords Series
Dragon Prince
Marked Prince
More Coming Soon!

To learn more about the Qurilixen World series of
books and to stay up to date on the latest book list
visit www.MichellePillow.com

AUTHOR UPDATES

To stay informed about when a new book in the
series installments is released, sign up for updates:

michellepillow.com/author-updates

To the Manfriend. Yes, you, Manfriend.
I'm kind of thinking that a book dedication should be
about equal to you bringing me a giant plate of pasta
for every book sold. Mmm, pasta. Oh, and dressed as—
why are you shaking your head at me?

NEW ORDER SOCIETY, DIMENSIONAL PLANE 303

LINNEA NEL EYED the bars of her cell. The New Order Society government wouldn't keep her locked up long. They never did. For every second she stayed in jail, the higher her offender ranking number would go. Since all number statistics were reported to the public, they would prefer she was ranked as a misdemeanor disturbance as opposed to anything major—like thievery or, worse, public chaos.

As one of the few people whose body's natural magnetism didn't allow for the anti-chaos implant, she was on every government and societal watch list. As a child, she'd managed to blend. Linnea had been a good student, a model participant in societal functions. Then came graduation. No higher learning institutes would take her. They didn't even bother to give her a good reason why she was rejected. Without an implant, they had no way of ensuring she did her own coursework and followed institutional policies. So it didn't matter how good she was or how smart. Unlike all other students, she would never be under their complete monitoring and control. They couldn't risk putting her into a position of power. They couldn't risk educating her. So she'd educated herself.

"Come on out of there, Nel," Orderkeeper Delkin said. The man should have instilled fear in her with his Goliath size, but Linnea had been in his cell way too many times. "And don't let us catch you in the library again without permission."

"Wouldn't dream of it," she answered dryly.

"Yeah," he muttered. "You know what to do. When you're checked out of the system, there's some people here waiting to talk to you."

People? Linnea frowned. Her own parents barely spoke to her—the uncontrollable one. Since she moved into New Order City, they hadn't really spoken to her. Why should they when her older brother and sister both did the family proud? Her genetic fluke only caused them embarrassment. To society's way of thinking, since she couldn't be watched, she was destined to cause trouble. She'd stopped trying to impress her parents years ago. Some battles couldn't be won, so there was no point in fighting them.

"See you next time around, keeper." Linnea typed in her identification number and made her way toward the front of the Orderkeeper Station. The tracking monitors made a familiar beep as she was scanned and found without a chip. They had tried making her wear a few around her neck, but her body's natural energy made them glitch. Once the monitor even read her as the wrong person—a dead singer, to be precise. That little event had raised a lot of alarms. There were still rumors that Silev had faked his own death and was really alive. What could she say? Diehard fans would believe anything. The only reason the orderkeepers didn't lock her up was because the authorities were fearful word of her condition would get out. Societal control depended on society trusting the implants implicitly.

"Linnea."

Linnea paused by the open door and slowly moved to stand in the doorway. Out of all the people who'd come to the station to get her, she never expected to see her sister. When they were little, Jinna had been her best friend. Now, looking at the woman, she couldn't see that little girl.

Instead, she saw the pristine and orderly counte-nance of Politician Nel, new leader of the anti-chaotic task force.

"Jin," Linnea answered. Like everyone else on the planet, her sister wore the one-piece suit. Mate-rial that belled around the legs led to tightly-fitted hips and a looser bodice. Her black hair had been streaked along the side with a bright, unnatural red, and tiny jewels had been adhered in a swirl pattern along the inside of it.

Linnea preferred to keep her black hair shorter with a streak of dark purple to match the purplish grey of her eyes. Her bodice was tight, less conserva-tive in design. A thick, black belt wrapped her ribs, dark purple over black material.

"Leave us," Jinna ordered her two guards. Linnea didn't back away as they passed, even as they stared at her like she was about to attack her own sister.

When they were alone, Linnea stepped into the room.

"This needs to stop," Jinna said. "I can't have a sister who's constantly being arrested for petty chaotic crimes."

"I'm great, thanks for asking, Jin," Linnea answered, moving to the long bench next to the wall. She took a seat and stretched her feet forward in easy repose. Smiling pleasantly, though she hardly felt pleasant, she inquired, "And you?"

"Always a child." Jinna frowned.

"Ah, Jin, I think you're being too hard on yourself. You've done well. I wouldn't call you a child." Linnea smirked. The look was a mask, a way of keeping the true depths of her hurt to herself. She wanted so badly to live a normal life, to have a family, find love and marry, have a career and a well-earned respect. Instead, she was arrested for daring to better herself.

"I didn't mean me," Jinna answered, flustered. "You are always a child. This proves my point. Do you ever think of anyone but yourself?"

Dropping all pretenses, Linnea drew her feet in and placed her elbows on her knees. "I was reading a book, not running naked through the streets."

"Not this time," Jinna grumbled.

"Once. I ran naked through the streets once. I was angry. You would be too if your application to medical learning was denied because of a stupid inability to take an implant. My grades were better than yours. I passed all my tests. I had recommendations and—"

"I'm not here to debate the past," Jinna interrupted.

"It's not the past," Linnea said. "It's my present, my future." She leaned over, jerking off her boot to expose her bare foot. A black numbered tattoo stared back at them, her identification number. Normally, the implants would be placed underneath the visible mark. Those numbers were everything—her money access, her education and work history, her purchasing rations, her identification. Everyone living in the New Order Society had a designation. When they were children, the government trucks had visited their school. The technicians wore costumes as to not frighten them. They danced and sang as the coded implants were injected beneath every child's number. Linnea's body rejected the implant, and every one after that. Her scarred foot attested to it. "It's not like I'm unwilling to be part of the system. I almost lost my foot to infection because I had the damned chip implanted too many times. I know the law. I know that this is the only way society can thrive. There must be order to chaos. You all just won't let me be a part of your society! It's not like I can help some natural electrical magnetism in my body—a current your doctors can't even define. Maybe if you let me go to school I could figure it out. I could design a better implant."

"Funding will not be granted to cure one person, Linnea. The needs of the many will be met first."

"The needs of the many? Like using chemists to make better-smelling grooming products?" Linnea wanted to scream, but knew that would do no good. "I could do that too."

"I'm here to discuss your future." When Jinna looked at her, Linnea didn't feel as if her sister actually saw her.

"You're letting me go to school?" Hope filled her.

"You know I can't do that."

The hope died. Though she should have been used to it by now, the disappointment physically hurt. "Then what?"

"I've secured a position for you with Dr. Cecilia Markos as an assistant." Jinna smiled for the first time.

"Assistant?"

"Don't look so disappointed. You clearly want to be in the medical field since you're constantly sneaking into the library to read medical textbooks."

"I read fiction too," Linnea said, just to be contrary. "Perhaps I really dream of being make-believe."

Even as part of her wanted to jump at the chance to be near medicine, another part knew that to be merely an assistant would eventually wear her down. To be so close and not be able to succeed. It would be torture.

"Dr. Cecilia Markos is fast becoming one of our greatest assets. You're lucky she's willing to take you with her."

"With her?" Linnea stood. "Where? Are you banishing me? New Order City is my home."

"Dr. Markos has been assigned to the off-plane program. You will be joining her on a trip through what we call the Divinity portal to a medically advanced dimensional plane in a parallel universe. It's primarily an ambassadorial journey, a basic trading of goodwill while gauging the plane's medical knowledge and their usefulness to our world."

"Portal travel?" Linnea felt a shiver work over her body. "I was joking when I said I wanted to be make-believe."

"When have you ever known me to joke?" Jinna arched a brow.

Good point.

"What do you mean a portal to a parallel universe?" she asked.

"Exactly that. You're smart, so I know I don't have to explain the concept of alternate realities and parallel universes to you. So take the theories you know and suppose they are real. Suppose someone found a way to move between the veils, so to speak. Looking at an alternate reality is like seeing our world if history had been altered in some way. Languages are similar, so you will not have a problem in that department. I'm told some people will look the same, but do not mistake them for being the same people. Humans will look like humans, save a few minor differences."

Linnea opened her mouth to speak, but said nothing. Jinna was serious.

"An entity called Divinity Corporation mastered the science of inter-dimensional travel. About two years ago they made contact with us. Since then, we've allowed a portal gate to be placed on our world. We're one of four-hundred-thirty-six charted universes, with infinitely more out there. We plan on staking a big claim in Divinity's project. Several ambassadors have been sent through and have come back successfully. Dr. Markos will lead the medical team. You will be her assistant."

Linnea frowned. "Team?"

"Well, a team of two. You and her."

"Why haven't I heard of this?"

"And cause societal panic? No. The public will not be made aware of these developments. There is no need to concern them. The government knows what is best for them."

"What if I say no? What if I tell? Your secret would be out."

Jinna laughed. "Do you still believe you can make people listen to you? Lin, Lin, Lin." Jinna shook her head in amusement. "You don't have a choice. You're going. It's what is best for societal harmony. I'm sure you understand."

"And when it's over? When I come back?" Linnea stiffened, a strange feeling of dread unfurling inside her. But, this was her sister. She didn't want to believe that Jinna would do something to hurt her.

"Why don't you concentrate your efforts on dealing with today? My guards have the information you need." Jinna left, leaving Linnea to stare after her. No matter how fantastic her sister's words were, Linnea found the idea of an alternate reality easier to believe than Jinna actually teasing her with this ridiculous conversation.

2

PORTAL TRAVEL WAS VERY real and Linnea had no choice but to experience it.

A pyramid roof set atop four square columns, which framed a platform. The columns were constructed of a dense material which created its own gravitational field and drew objects to it. They hid a complex configuration of liquid crystals, electrical currents, mirrors and vacuums. It was held in check by the wavelength of a specific blue light, which kept the portal inactive. Should the light change, a dimensional shift would occur, taking whoever stood on the platform to a new parallel universe.

"In the early days, before these platforms, plane travel had been a matter of trial and error. Many testers died when they materialized inside solid objects," Politician Shinclus said, his eyes on the Divinity portal. The man smiled, a large, almost toadlike expression. When he spoke, his great lips smacked together as if about to strike with his tongue at any moment. "Now they use microscopic probes before sending people through, so accidents are rare."

Linnea's eyes grew wide as she looked at the politician. She found herself unconsciously stepping away from him.

"Is my sister...?" Linnea paused. She hadn't seen her sister since the jail. In fact, she hadn't heard from any of her family, though she'd tried contacting them. "Is Politician Nel here?"

"No. She does not oversee this project," he said, and dismissed her question. Then, motioning back to the platform that was the center point of his story, he continued on as if she hadn't spoken. "It is not too late to change your mind." His smile widened. It wasn't the first time a man had looked at Linnea in such a way— eyes narrowed, lips parted, chest filling with heavy breath. "Other...arrangements could be made for you."

"Dr. Markos is expecting me. We've already discussed—"

"Other assistants can be arranged. There is no

need for you to travel to another dimension." His eyes dipped over her chest, lingering on the tighter fit of her black bodice.

"I have reason to go."

"I can give your reason to stay. My home is quite large."

"It's a medical plane." Linnea lowered her eyes to the floor and lied, "I have hopes that they'll be able to cure...my...feminine..." She glanced up briefly, forcing a blush over her features.

Politician Shinclus cleared his throat. "Oh, yes, well, I haven't been through the portal myself, but I'm told it's quite an enjoyable ride." Motioning to a nearby woman, he said, "Here is the material Dr. Markos has requested."

Linnea took the stack of papers, glancing at the top. They were a compilation of basic medicines and known diseases.

"There is Dr. Markos. I must see if she requires me for anything before we leave." All too glad to have a reason to leave the lecherous politician's side, Linnea tried not to laugh as she hurried away. Shinclus apparently didn't like her enough to risk contracting a social illness. Then, seeing Dr. Markos, her smile faded. She didn't like the woman. Like everyone else, she was judgmental and a little conde-scending.

Dr. Markos wore a red, one-piece suit. The sleeves were long, falling past the woman's hands. Her brunette hair was all one color and had been pulled back from her face. Her features seemed overly pale in the blue light reflecting off the portal. When the woman looked at her, Linnea said, half conversationally, half to get a rise out of the fine doctor, "You know, Politician Shinclus told me that people sometimes get rematerialized into solid objects when going through these things."

"He was just trying to scare you," Dr. Markos answered tersely. "Politician Shinclus is known for his bad humor. It is true accidents happened in the past, but that is why they send out the probes first. Besides, where we are going is a known destination and an opposite portal will receive us on the other side. Everyone there works for the central hospital government in some capacity. It should be like going to a giant hospital." She turned to study Linnea. The blue light from the portal reflected in the woman's eyes. "Weren't you supposed to change your hair?"

"I didn't make it to my appointment. Something else came up." Linnea arched a brow and shifted the papers in her arms. Drawling sarcastically, she added, "I don't really think it matters all that much. I'm sure they'll make allowance for our alien customs."

Cecilia closed her eyes, appearing annoyed. "The plane we're traveling to does not know of our fashion customs. We might unintentionally insult them. Did you read the recommendations report put together by the Committee for Interplane Diplomacy?"

"I was going to," Linnea drawled, "but I was in the middle of a different book at the time. I wanted to finish it before we left."

Cecilia frowned, saying, "It's too late to do anything about your hair now. We will be leaving soon."

Linnea mimicked the woman's disapproving expression. The unspoken meaning in the doctor's tone was clear—her hair ultimately didn't matter because Linnea was only her assistant, a nonconformist, not a doctor.

Workers began filing out of the room. A low, steady hum sounded moments before a voice could be heard overhead, ordering, "Dr. Markos, Citizen Nel, please report to the platform."

3

CITY OF ASCLEPIUS, COUNTRY OF
CHIRON, DIMENSIONAL PLANE 187

Dr. Samuel Swift didn't move from his place on
the narrow cot. The room was small, but he wouldn't
be disturbed. It was practically the only room within
the walls of the Central Hospital and Optimal
Health Centre where he could find any kind of sanc-
tuary and, if he was lucky, a few minutes of sleep.

As Director of Central Hospital, Sam had one
person to answer to—the Medical Supreme. Unfortunately, Medical Supreme Walter had been especially
demanding lately—not the least of which was using
his laboratories in the middle of the night, something
that required Sam's special clearance and attendance
within the building.

Exhaustion and stress filled him from just
thinking about it. He didn't like Supreme Walter's

late night experimenting and he especially didn't like not knowing what those experiments were. But, his position was a delicate one. The Medical Supreme was in charge of funding and had power. To question him would be to lose not only his position, but his hospital's funding. With only a cheating former wife to call family, this hospital was all he had.

The former wife was pretty, he'd allow her that much. He'd been blinded by her physical charms—round breasts, soft flesh, thighs that would part as eagerly as her mouth. She'd sucked her way into his life, quite literally. Shamefully, that's what he missed most—not her, but the feel of her, the companionship, the release.

A light beep sounded. One of the benefits of living on one of the most medically advanced planes of existence was the constant monitoring of health. The room monitors constantly checked his system, anticipating his needs. Automatically turning his head to the side, he let the injector extending from the wall give him a shot in the neck. Instantly, his stress levels lessened and he felt better.

Another beep sounded and he opened one eye. He reached for his waistband a little too eagerly, tugging at it to pull his pants off his hips. The computer had sensed his borderline arousal and was instructing him to take care of it. Who was he to argue with science?

Sighing, he wrapped his fingers around his cock. No one in particular came to mind as he lazily stroked himself. Though he enjoyed it, he knew it was merely a physical function like eating or breathing. He'd heard of people finding great passion. Though he'd enjoyed the charms of his former wife, he hadn't felt any kind of mighty love passion. Through the Divinity portal, they had traded research with a plane of people who'd done extensive mapping of the brain. Emotions were easy enough to explain, read, even cure. Love was merely what they had called phenylethylamine, a trick of the brain, a chemical the body produced to create the emotion.

He found his mind trying to wander to work, to the mental checklist of things to be done. Off-world doctors were coming today. He'd have to greet and acclimate them. There would be tests to run, scans, checkups. Then he would be expected to escort them to whichever facility he deemed best for their trading purposes.

He glanced down his body, stroking harder. The dry rub of his hand on flesh caused his stomach to tighten. His breathing deepened. Pleasure rippled over him. So close. Almost... Almost—

"Dr. Swift, the dignitaries have arrived. They are in decontamination," Dr. Lu's voice interrupted. The man was the last person he wanted to hear at that moment. The shock of it jolted him back from his release. Though some substance did leak from the tip, the pressure remained inside his stomach.

With a frustrated sigh, he reached for the wall panel and pressed a button to answer, "Dr. Lu, I'll be there in a moment. Please see that they are cleared."

"Dr. Fauchet has already been dispatched to see to it," Lu answered.

"Very good." Sam took a deep breath before getting up to clean himself off. The wall panel beeped a reminder that he needed to do something about his levels. Unfortunately duty called and he hit an override code to ignore his current state of un-release for the time being.

As he was the director, the incident would not be reported to the others. It was one of the small perks of the job, a little bit of medical privacy. If the others knew how many times he ended up taking matters into his own hands without the aid of female companionship, they'd probably stage an intervention. Though, finding women in his position was hard. He didn't want them fucking him because he had power. He didn't want them thinking they *had* to fuck with him because he had power. The Medical Supreme didn't seem to have the same issue with power that Sam had. The man would seduce anyone he wanted—the more unattainable, the better. In fact, the Medical Supreme even hinted at using the Divinity portal to bring through virgins for their trainable pleasure. His cock tightened at the erotic idea of tight female flesh to plunge into. However, he found the Medical Supreme a letch. Sure, the idea of sexual vessels worked well for a healthy fantasy to get off when he was alone, but the reality of importing virgins was a sort of mental pathogen he wanted no part of. Fantasy women wanted to be fucked. Real women deserved the choice.

Besides, he never understood the obsession some men had with virgins. He hadn't held on to his own virginity, why should the women who came to his bed be expected to? Sam found himself pulling aside his lab coat and reaching to stroke his cock through his pants. And, furthermore, he didn't want to have to train his lover to fuck him. He had enough work to do as it was.

The reminder of work caused him to growl and drop the coat. The long length of the standard-issue facility uniform, a long blue coat with red trim, would hide his erection until it lost interest. Since he was expected to escort the visitors to a facility several hours outside the city, it would be a long while before he had a chance to take care of himself properly. The idea did nothing to his mood as he grumpily reached for a medical clipboard and hit his hand against the door scanner.

4

QUITE AN ENJOYABLE RIDE.

As the color of the light shifted to a pale green to pull Linnea through the portal, she cursed Politician Shinclus for his obvious lie. The pain of portal travel was unimaginable. The humming in her ears grew louder, drowning out all other sounds. Linnea closed her eyes to the bright light. She wanted to scream, but when she opened her mouth it felt as if her jaw was being ripped away from her skull. Flesh burned and her entire body was ripped apart at a molecular level. She should have been dead, or unconscious, but her mind stayed completely aware.

Those few seconds of pain were unlike anything she'd ever experienced. Then it was over, leaving her body numb and weak. She collapsed onto the hard platform, dropping her papers and not caring. She gasped for breath, coughing and choking as her lungs filled with a sickeningly sweet air.

Quite an enjoyable ride?

Bedlam and anarchy!

She was vaguely aware of Cecilia Markos on the floor next to her. The pale green turned to blue and her hearing came back in the form of loud, blaring alarms. Linnea covered her sensitive ears. "So loud!"

"Sterilization commencing," a male voice announced, louder than the alarm. "Please stand and move away from the platform."

Linnea didn't bother looking up. She crawled forward to gather the papers before pushing to her feet. Cecilia stayed on the ground, shaking. Reaching down, Linnea pulled the woman up by her arm.

"Please stand and move away from the platform," the voice repeated, even louder. No one was there. The voice came from a sound system. She looked around but couldn't see any viewing devices looking in at them. The room was constructed of shiny metal —from the floors to the walls to the ceilings.

"I think that's us," Linnea yelled over the alarm, not letting go of Cecilia's arm as they moved, afraid one of them would collapse again and injure themselves. They both turned, startled, watching as a shield slid down from the ceiling, blocking the platform.

"Welcome, dignitaries from the New Order Society, Dimensional Plane 303, to Central Hospital and Optimal Health Centre in the City of Asclepius, Country of Chiron, Dimensional Plane 187. We are now scanning you for foreign dimensional parasites and viruses. Please do not move until scanning is complete." A series of lights followed the male's orders, flashing over them. The alarms thankfully stopped. "Sterilization complete. Please state your clearance code."

"Dr. Cecilia Markos," her companion answered. "New Order Society dignitary."

"This is tedious," Linnea muttered. Her ears still rang from the blaring noise. "I hope they don't all talk that loud."

"Voice recognition accepted. Please move to the orange door." A metallic gray door with a series of numbers and letters written in orange across the front opened automatically and they passed through to the metallic gray corridors of the hospital. They stepped down the hall, not sure where they were going, but heading down the longest route. The orange letters on the wall seemed to indicate some kind of navigational system, but they weren't trained to read it.

"It's only for a couple of months," Cecilia said under her breath.

"Yeah," Linnea answered, "but two months of what?"

A man appeared in a long blue coat with red trim holding an electronic device in his hands. The device held his attention for a long moment. The women stopped, waiting for him to look up and give them some sort of indication as to what they should do next. Linnea shared a quick look with Cecilia, but the there was no camaraderie between their gazes. In truth, Cecilia was as much a stranger to Linnea as the man standing before them.

"Welcome," the man stated. "Welcome, doctors."

"I'm the doctor, Dr. Cecilia Markos," Cecilia answered, her tone clipped and frankly a little insulting. She motioned to Linnea. "This is my assistant, Linnea Nel."

Linnea gave a rueful smile at the other woman's introduction and suddenly regretted bothering to help her up off the floor. She had hoped, being from the same dimensional plane, Cecilia would show her some form of respect. Though why Linnea expected as much was a mystery even to her. She was used to people treating her poorly, and all because of a stupid tiny-little implant.

"Welcome, Dr. Markos, Sans Nel," the man amended. He smiled at both of them equally, unfazed by her non-doctor status. Linnea was inclined to like him instantly.

Cecilia nodded once.

"Thank you," Linnea answered politely.

"I am Dr. Gerard Fauchet. I will be your guide while you're on our plane. Anything you need, all you have to do is ask." He motioned to the papers. "Would you like me to carry that for you?"

"No, I've got it." Linnea glanced pointedly at Cecilia and added, "I am the assistant, after all."

"We don't work with parchment, but I can have one of the doctors scan your documents into a clipboard if you like." He lifted his electronic device to indicate what he was talking about. "In fact, I understand supplies are waiting for us at the assigned research facility."

Cecilia looked around, clearly taken aback. "You mean...we will not be working here? Near the portal?"

Linnea had the same question. A thin thread of fear worked through her at the idea. Of course, she knew this was part of her mission, but the nagging idea that her plane might just abandon her here wouldn't leave her. They couldn't kill her. They couldn't monitor her. But they could trap her in an alternate reality and tell her family she'd suffered an accident. Who wouldn't believe it? Inter-dimensional travel just sounded dangerous. And that was if they even admitted to what they'd done to her. Her family might not even know she'd gone missing. They might even be relieved to never hear from her again.

"Afraid we might keep you here against your will?" Gerard teased. Linnea couldn't help but return the man's playful smile. However, Cecilia was far from amused. The open expression disappeared from the man's face. In a more subdued tone, he stated, "Please, follow me."

Linnea gave her companion a questioningly glance as Gerard led them down the hall. She caught the woman staring at the man's ass. This was who they sent as the dignitary? A displeased woman who lusted after the first male specimen they came across? Linnea gave a small laugh, feeling a tiny bit superior to the great Dr. Markos.

Cecilia began to cough.

"Doctor?" Gerard inquired, glancing at his clipboard then the women.

Cecilia touched her chest lightly. "I am still adapting to the air."

"It smells like we're walking near a confectionary," Linnea observed politely, trying to lighten the insulting tilt to Cecilia's words. This was getting ridiculous. As unhappy as she was by her plane's anti-chaos laws keeping her out of medical higher learning, she didn't want her people misrepresented by the rude doctor at her side. "The air is very sweet."

"That is the air-filtering sterilizer," Gerard said. "The air is continuously tested for abnormalities and purified. You have nothing to fear here. We haven't had a serious illness for, well, some would argue for centuries now, depending on your particular definition of serious." He waved his hand toward the ceiling. "I am told that after a time you will become accustomed to the scent. We tried modifying the formula to be unscented, but it lost two-point-three percent potency."

"No illness for so long?" Cecilia questioned, clearly trying to convey the significance of such a discovery when she looked at Linnea. "That is quite the accomplishment."

Linnea didn't react. Of course that was why they were here—to glean medical knowledge to cure diseases on their plane. She didn't believe for a second Jinna merely wanted them to spread some goodwill and come home.

Gerard led them through the hall, turning several times until it became apparent the halls were an endless maze that would be impossible to navigate without a map. Linnea noticed monitors on the wall displayed their life signs as they passed, and if she walked too close to them they blipped, so she tried to stay toward the center of the hall. She stopped walking, staring at the monitor, trying to decipher what it was saying.

"Ah, Dr. Fauchet." The abrupt sound cut into her thoughts and directed her attention to the arrogant sounding man coming down the hall.

"Dr. Markos, Sans Nel," Gerard introduced, "may I present Medical Supreme Walter, his son Dr. Sebastjan Walter and Dr. Walter's wife, Sans Ariella."

"Doctor," the Medical Supreme acknowledged, glancing only briefly at Linnea. He had a smooth, youthful look to him that contrasted the intelligence in his blue eyes. A foreshadowing of gray salted the black hair at his temples.

"Welcome," Dr. Walter said. Ariella simply

nodded and didn't look at any one person for too long.

Linnea noted that everyone talked louder on this plane, as if someone turned up the volume a couple notches. She was tempted to rub her ears, but refrained.

"And this is the hospital coordinator Dr. Lu," Gerard finished. Dr. Lu stayed back behind the others, more interested in his clipboard than his visitors.

"Welcome to Asclepius," the Medical Supreme said. "We look forward to a mutual exchange of knowledge. I have chosen Dr. Fauchet to be your guide. He will remain at your side. Should you need anything, please speak directly to him or to Dr. Swift. I will be unable to attend you at the research facility. I am a very busy man after all."

Cecilia began to answer, but the Medical Supreme cut her off.

"Here he is!" The Medical Supreme lifted his hand, motioning behind them. "May I present the esteemed Dr. Swift, Director of Central Hospital."

Linnea couldn't move. All thoughts left her as Dr. Swift moved closer to join their group. He nodded in acknowledgement. Dark brown hair framed his tanned face and green eyes. The cut seemed long compared to the other natives, but the look suited him. Well, honestly, she wasn't sure if the look suited *him*, but it suited *her* just fine. Attraction rocketed through her body, causing her nerves to come alive. It was potent and raw, as if he emitted some kind of sex pheromone all over her body. She shifted uncomfortably, her one-piece jumpsuit feeling very tight and oddly erotic. Moisture wetted her sex.

Linnea took a deep breath and pressed the papers closer to her chest. Her breasts ached in appreciation of the gesture, wanting to be rubbed. Unable to help herself, she stared at his strong features—deep eyes, proud nose, deliciously firm lips. As a highly trained doctor he probably knew all the right nerve bundles to touch inside a woman's body to make her orgasm. Damn, it had been way too long since she'd had sex.

And then she noticed his expression. It was one of disdain as he stared a long time at her hair. She resisted the urge to touch the purple streak. As quickly as it came, her desire left, replaced by irritation and indignation.

"Dr. Markos," Dr. Swift acknowledged, turning his attention from Linnea without bothering to greet her. Sebastjan slipped away with his wife, followed by Dr. Lu. "I've ordered your transport readied. Your belongings have already been loaded. Dr. Fauchet will show you where to go." He glanced at Linnea and shifted his weight. "I must attend to a few matters here but will join you later at the facility."

"Sans Nel has parchment to be transferred to a clipboard. Perhaps she should work here and arrive later with you when she is finished?" Gerard suggested.

Dr. Swift didn't spare her a look as he nodded stiffly. "Very well. Sans Nel, follow me. I will show you where you can work."

Cecilia gestured that Linnea should follow the man. Frowning, she had no choice but to go after the arrogant doctor.

"Where did my son...?" The Medical Supreme began to question, glancing around as Linnea passed by him. "Excuse me. I have urgent business to attend to."

With a few turns of the corners, Linnea found herself alone with Dr. Arrogant. The man didn't look at her and she couldn't help but think this was going to be a very long couple of months.

5

HIS DICK HATED HIM.

Sam tried to take deep breaths without being noticeable. Unfortunately, his uncompleted desires only grew more painful the second he looked at the visiting dignitary. Hell, by all rights he should have been attracted to Dr. Markos, the educated, tall, polished off-plane doctor. Instead, his cock pointed directly at her Sans assistant, Linnea Nel. Linnea didn't even have normal colored hair, or eyes—at least as they knew it on his plane. The shoulder-length black locks were streaked with dark purple and her eyes were a strange shade of purplish-grey. He found himself fascinated by their uniqueness.

Sam hated Dr. Fauchet.

At least, for the moment he did. The man's very

reasonable assertion that Linnea transfer her parchments before transport made sense. It was protocol to enter new off-plane information into the universal database as quickly as possible.

However, reason aside, he did not want to be alone with this woman, not until he had a chance to finish masturbating. Even now he wanted to unwrap her slender body and discover what other strange colorings she carried. Was her nether hair streaked with purple as well? Did the color occur naturally? What about her nipples? Would they match the glossy color of her lips?

He almost walked past their turn and had to abruptly stop.

Linnea stumbled behind him. He turned and gestured to the door. "You may work in here."

She blinked those damn unique eyes as she looked into the room and then back at him. "Perhaps I should stick with parchment."

"I'll show you how to use the clipboard. The functions are quite easy."

"I'm not worried about figuring out the functions so much as inadvertently crashing your system." Linnea adjusted the stack of papers against her chest to free one of her arms. She lifted it and moved closer to the wall monitor. The screen blipped once, twice, before suddenly flashing faster the closer she came to the unit until the words were unrecognizable. When she pulled away, it went back to normal. "There is a reason my plane sent me with paper copies."

"Interesting," Sam said, studying her. Without thought, he reached to touch her free arm. She felt like he expected a woman to feel—warm and soft. "I don't remember seeing this phenomenon before."

Linnea's eyes dropped to his hand. "I'm not dangerous to people, just electronics."

"A rare condition," Sam agreed. He let go, not trusting himself to continue touching her. "Come with me. Let's see what we can do to counteract your affliction while you are here."

"Affliction," she repeated softly, not sounding too pleased.

Sam led her toward one of the private examination rooms. The square space looked like many of the rooms in the hospital, complete with a scanning booth. The door automatically shut behind them as they entered. "This is a medical booth. When you step on the platform, thin lights will come out and record your body's readings. It won't hurt."

"That's what they said about the Divinity portal." Linnea set her stack of papers on a metal counter. "That thing felt as if it ripped me apart. It will be much harder to step into the portal a second time, knowing what's coming."

"We can give you something for the pain before you leave to make it easier." Sam eyed her back. The tight material of her one-piece suit hugged her curves. Curiosity got the better of him, and he said, "It will be optimal if you remove your clothing for the scanners to get cleaner readings."

Linnea stiffened.

What was he doing? Okay, so technically it was true, but the accuracy difference only amounted to exactly point-two-percent.

"Lovely," she drawled, though the sound of her voice belied the definition of the word as he knew it. "Just like the Orderkeeper logs back home."

"Orderkeeper?" he questioned.

"Anti-chaos department." The answer was hardly helpful.

Linnea began undressing, her back toward him. She pulled the cinch from her waist and placed it next to the papers on the counter. Sam gripped his clipboard, watching the unveiling of her body. He tried to assure himself it was medical curiosity—a visual comparison of off-plane anatomy. His cock begged to differ with his motives. Fuck, it actually throbbed.

The clothing slipped off her shoulders to unveil smooth skin. A long valley ran down along her spine, shifting as she freed her arms. Slowly, she turned.

What color were her nipples? The question tickled his mind. He swallowed, desperate to find out the answer. Momentarily disappointed when they were not some strange shade, he quickly recovered. The large pink tips were perfect, punctuating two shapely handfuls. His eyes followed her clothing, down, over hips, down, over legs, down...

Sam breathed deeply before glancing up to meet her eyes. She stared at him, a brow arched. Unable to think of a better excuse for his unprofessionalism, he said stiffly, "You appear compatible with my plane. The machine should not have a problem reading you. Please, step into the booth for scanning."

The lasers turned on as she approached. She gave a small jump back before holding out her hand to touch the light. Obviously deciding it wasn't harmful, she went inside.

"Just stand still. It will only take a few moments." Sam watched the lights dancing on her flesh, touching where he wanted to. She stared at the wall in front of her, not moving, barely breathing. He wanted to say more to her, but was unsure how to start a conversation with a Sans woman from another plane.

Sam had never been sexually aroused by a scan before. The only explanation was he'd come into the situation already denied release. What he was feeling was simple physical need. By the looks of this woman they would have nothing in common on an intellectual level. He liked being a doctor and talking about medical things. When he spoke to a Sans, he didn't have much to say beyond the required niceties.

A loud blare sounded overhead, dragging him from his thoughts. Surprised, he turned his attention to the woman in the booth. Her wide eyes looked at him and she covered her stomach protectively with her hands.

"Containment," the automated system announced, as a plastic wall slid down from the ceiling, trapping her on one side of the room. "Containment. Exam One. Terminal. Containment. Security level one. Containment."

Needlessly, Sam looked at the door. They were in Exam Twenty. The alarm wasn't for Linnea. Who was in the hospital? Protocol demanded all exams for the day be cancelled due to the arriving dignitaries. Unless...

"What's happening? What's wrong with me?" Linnea asked.

"It's not you," Sam answered. The door had automatically locked at the containment alarm and he quickly punched in his twenty-five digit override code. "Stay here. Get dressed. I'll come back for you. There is nothing to worry about. This hospital is full of doctors who know what to do."

"But—" The slamming door behind him cut off her words. He hurried through the large facility.

The automated message repeated. "Containment. Exam One. Terminal. Containment."

The closer he got to Exam One, the stronger the sweet scent of sanitizer became. About halfway to Exam One, he met with Supreme Walter. The man gave him a hard look and stated, "Don't you have a dignitary to escort?"

Sam was taken aback by the man's tone. "But..."

"It's a false alarm. I'm taking care of it. All exams have been cancelled for the day, you know that." As if catching himself, the Medical Supreme took a deep breath and instantly changed his sour expression into that of a politician. "Please, see to our guests. We don't want them frightened by this alarm, do we? I'll make sure Dr. Lu gives you a full report of the incident."

As the director, Sam wanted to protest, but there was nothing he could say when given an order directly from the Medical Supreme, especially when he had no justifiable reason as to why he should disobey and check the incident for himself. He nodded. "Of course. We leave immediately and I will be back by the end of the day. I'll expect his report on my return."

Supreme Walter quickly stepped away, leaving Sam to watch after him with suspicion. As he made his way back to Linnea, the alarms stopped. He relaxed a little, suddenly glad he hadn't pushed the issue with the Medical Supreme as he'd instinctively wanted to. They would not have turned off the alarms if it had been a real incident. He stopped at the wall panel, typed in his code and ordered a hospital-wide equipment check. The staff would hate him for it, but it needed to be done. He couldn't have alarms misfiring and scaring people.

When he returned to Linnea, he found her standing several feet back from a wall monitor, studying it. She didn't look directly at him. "Did the mighty doctors take care of it?"

He paused, unable to help himself as he glanced at her ass in the tight pants she wore. They left nothing to his imagination. Knowing she probably didn't understand the monitor as she wasn't a medical professional, he said, "There is nothing to be concerned over. It was an alarm test that should not have been scheduled when off-world dignitaries were on site."

She glanced at him and back at the wall. "Did my scan tell you anything?"

"Of course." He went to the medical scanner's controls and began scrolling through the information. A two-dimensional image of her naked outline appeared. Damn, he even found that sexy. Suddenly he was grateful for transport sleep. Otherwise it would be a very long, secluded drive to the facility to drop her off.

He paused, staring at her basic readings. They were off just a fraction, but enough to cause an anomaly. Curiously, he had never seen such a reading before, but it was the only thing he could find that might have such a side effect.

"Well?" she prompted when he didn't speak.

Sam blinked, realizing he was again staring at her naked outline in the charts. He typed in a quick prescription and then closed the file. "I can give you something that should help, but for a permanent solution I'll need to do more tests."

"Do you know what it is?"

"Yes, I understand your readings. I'll give you medicine that will help."

"What kind of readings? What kind of medicine?" she persisted.

"I understand you may be frightened, being in a new plane, but rest assured we know what we are doing." Sam went to the wall unit to retrieve the syringe he'd ordered, along with a medical chip necklace.

"I didn't ask if you knew what you were doing." Linnea sounded irritated with him and he wondered at it. "I asked what you were doing so I could know what you are going to do to my body."

"I'm giving you medicine. Something to help." He handed her the necklace. How could he explain complicated internal medicine to her in a way she'd understand? "Put this on."

"It's lovely, thank you." She did, albeit slowly. "So you think you can permanently fix me?"

He lifted the shot to her neck and stuck it in.

"Ow!" She jerked in surprise and quickly wrapped her fingers over the injection site. "What was that?"

"A shot to help alleviate your symptoms. This first one should take a few hours to work fully. After that, if you notice any electronic glitches, use the necklace to refill an injection by pressing to a monitor screen. The first shot should last you a long while."

"So you can't permanently fix me?"

"I might be able to, but I don't want to alter your genetics until I've had ample time to look over any side effects that might arise." He gave her a slight smile, trying to ease her fears "We wouldn't want you growing extra limbs."

Her eyes widened, clearly thinking he was serious. She took a small step back and he saw her arms stiffen as if she expected something to happen to them. "And the shot?"

"Temporary measure." Sam gave up any attempts at joking. He wasn't sure what had brought the inappropriate behavior on in the first place. "If you notice any side effects, report them to a local doctor."

"Not you?" She rubbed her neck as if he'd done her some great injury. "But you're the one who gave it to me."

"If I am around, yes, I will do. However any of the local doctors will be able to access your charts." The room felt small and the idea of seeing much more of her had a very uncomfortable effect on his body. He turned abruptly to the door. "We should go. They'll be expecting us at the biosphacility."

6

LINNEA FOLLOWED the rude doctor out of the exam room and through the maze halls of the Central Hospital and Optimal Health Centre. Her neck was sore, and she didn't appreciate the surprise attack. A little warning would have been nice. A lot of explanation would have been better. Still, as she passed a wall monitor she noticed they didn't blink nearly as badly. Now, if she could manage not to grow any extra body parts, this could be a good thing for her. She fingered the necklace he'd given her. The purple stone matched her eyes. She thought that an interesting coincidence. At least it wasn't bright yellow or something obnoxious. The round stone looked like a rock, but apparently it held the code to her medicine inside.

If he could cure her, that meant she could get the chip. She could be tracked. A smile spread over her face. She could go to school. Her parents would stop making excuses about her. They'd invite her back to family functions. She'd be included.

Did she dare hope?

A bright light shone and she looked to see Dr. Swift walking through the front doors of the hospital. She momentarily forgot her medical condition as she looked at the new world. Linnea wasn't sure what she expected to see, but somehow this wasn't it. The planet, so far, appeared to be constructed of stone. The Central Hospital and Optimal Health Centre dominated the area. Thick columns and oversized stone arches mimicked the smaller surrounding buildings. The outside architecture was nothing like the metal corridors within. The stone façade of the hospital joined the smooth stone of the empty streets, growing into a carved stone landscape. The streets, sidewalks and buildings seemed connected by one smooth formation of rock. Statues set on the ground and their stiff lines and symmetrical features were just as clean and orderly as the surrounding buildings. The only visible pieces of life, besides the two people walking toward the transport, were the small plants encased in large glass boxes.

"Where is it?" Sam said under his breath. He looked back and forth along the empty street.

"Perhaps your driver is running behind?" she offered.

He gave her a look that kind of made her feel like an idiot. She arched a brow at him and pretended not to care about his opinion. As a non-doctor, she wasn't going to be afforded much respect in this world. That was fine. She didn't get a lot of respect on her world either. She would simply keep her mouth shut, absorb as much information as she could, and hope for a cure that would change everything.

"I'm not an imbecile, you know." Linnea wasn't sure what prompted her to speak of it. She rubbed her neck. "You don't have to talk down to me or simplify things so I can understand them."

He didn't answer.

"Finally." Sam stepped toward the street as a large box hovered its way toward them. Linnea leaned over, looking under the vehicle. It didn't touch the ground. When she stood straight, her companion was staring at her.

"Interesting mechanics," she said, dismissingly. Though, in truth, she wanted to ask him how it worked.

"If you like transporter mechanics." The doctor stepped inside the vehicle and disappeared within.

Linnea leaned in to look inside before stepping up the small steps that had appeared by the door. She found him seated in the near-empty space and slowly took a seat across from him. "How do you drive it?"

"Transporters drive themselves. The coordinates have already been programmed." Sam pressed a button and the door shut, sealing them in. Linnea leaned toward a window and looked out. There was no way to open the window for fresh air.

"What is your city called?" she asked, trying to make conversation. The vehicle was deafeningly silent, a strange contrast to the loud voices and equipment.

"Asclepius."

The vehicle began to move soundlessly, hovering over the earth as it self-navigated streets. It sped by quickly, making it impossible for her to focus on the passing building. She saw a few people, dressed like the doctor across from her, but they didn't pay any attention to the woman staring out at them.

"You might want to get comfortable," he said. "It's a long trip."

She took the hint and stopped gawking out of the window. Instead she looked at him. She opened her mouth to ask more questions, but a strange hissing sound came from the transport. She stiffened in her seat. Light smoke filtered in from the walls. Linnea covered her mouth, panicking. She stood, automatically reaching for the window. Unable to open it, she turned toward the door. It was over in moments. Her limbs became heavy, and as she turned she lost control of her body. She landed on her knees. Kneeling on the floor, she tried to stand but her body would not obey. Her eyes widened and she found her face falling toward Sam's lap.

7

SAM FOUGHT the urge to awaken. His body was tired, his mind half-aware. The drugging effects of transport sleep did not concern him, but his brain should not be trying to wake his body.

The transport turned, swaying him. He felt pressure in his lap. That pressure felt like a dream. He gave a soft moan. The transport turned again. Something rocked against his cock like an erotic fantasy. Not fully aware, he reached to rub at his hard dick. His fingers instead met with soft hair. The contact caused her head to move on his lap. Who was he to deny the dream? He automatically tugged at his coat, lifting it out of her way. Oh, but his body needed this. He then fumbled for his waistband, tugging at it, freeing the head of his cock. He felt soft fingers and pulled them with his hand into his pants. They touched his arousal and he gave another moan before the drugged sleep overtook the growing pleasure.

LINNEA'S HEAD bumped up and down in a steady rhythm. She inhaled deeply, caught in a haze of sleep. Her body ached, but it was a dull pain, far away and hardly noticeable. A new smell filled her as she breathed, erotically pleasant. It was an intimate smell, one she didn't readily know but one she wasn't too eager to escape. Her head bumped again, bouncing faster. She flexed her hand. Her fingers were moist and hot and trapped. Her elbow pointed out to the side. Smooth, firm skin pressed into her palm. Slowly, she became aware that her thumb and forefinger were gripping the base of a penis next to a man's balls.

Was she having sex? Had she drank too much and passed out on the guy? Her head bobbed again, the movement matching the man's press up into her hand. She blinked open her eyes, seeing blue material bunched by her face and little else. Her hand delved down the front of the guy's pants, her fingers wrapped around a very nice specimen of male virility. The intimate smell became stronger. She breathed deeper, opening her mouth. Her breath hit the shaft. Desire stung through her. Somehow, without her realizing it, her pussy had responded and was soaking her pants with a damp response. Automatically, without thought in her hazed state, she did what came naturally in such a situation and she stroked the thick cock. Damn, but it felt huge.

"Fuck," a man whispered at her bolder strokes. Hands grabbed her hair and pulled her head closer. Her lips hit the shaft and the man groaned in approval. "Fuck."

Before she could fully comprehend that she should even stop to think about what was happening, she had her mouth open and a thick cock being shoved inside. The man held her head and pressed his hips up, nearly choking her in his eagerness.

"Ah, fuck," he groaned. His legs stirred beneath her. She fell to the side, bumping her shoulder against the wall of the transport. Weakly, she braced herself with her hands as she became aware of the hard press of the transport floor against her knees. A dull pain slowly grew in intensity, radiating up her legs. She blinked again, fighting for consciousness.

"Don't stop...what the...?" A more alert tone entered the man's surprised voice.

Linnea glanced up, instantly becoming aware of where she was and who she was with. She pulled back and he let her head go. Her lips made a smacking noise as they left Dr. Swift's cock.

His glassy eyes blinked as if he fought to awaken fully. Conscious thought did not alleviate the aching in her sex. She tasted him on her tongue. Hands reached for her, tugging at her shirt to free her breasts. Time made little sense to her fogged brain. Linnea wasn't sure how, but she was suddenly naked and straddling Dr. Swift on the seat. His glassy eyes met hers and he blinked heavily. His cock bumped her pussy, missing entrance. It took several tries but they finally managed to correct the aim. He jerked her down on his lap and groaned loudly. Linnea gasped, the surprise of his large fit causing her to find a bit of reason. What was happening? Why was she straddling Dr. Swift? Why was he letting her? The last thing she remembered was his irritatingly superior look. Then smoke. Then...

He lifted her by her waist and jerked her down hard, going deeper. She inhaled sharply. The man was strong, able to control her with his hands. She braced herself on his shoulders. His eyes closed and he used her hips to make her fuck him. There was nothing sweet and tender about the way he lifted her up and then slammed her down onto his cock. Oh, but it was gratifying. She pressed her stomach forward to create a more pleasurable angle. Linnea let him fuck her.

"What are you doing?" he asked, confused, even as his hips thumped up into her. Sam made a loud animalistic noise and flipped her over onto the seat. His cock left her for the briefest of moments. Her back hit the slick material. Sam came over her, braced his arms, and began pumping his hips harder than before. The new position allowed him to go deeper. "Oh fuck, your pussy is..."

His incoherent mumblings were drowned out by the sound of her climax. She cried out as her orgasm hit her. Sam's release joined hers and he tensed over her.

For a long time she didn't move, only drifted between the haze of aftermath and the fog of drugged sleep. It would have been so easy to fall back into oblivion. The man above her shifted. She blinked heavily and pushed up from the seat.

Reason came back to her slowly, but when it finally dawned on her what she'd done, the truth hit hard. She'd fucked Dr. Swift.

Her knees ached as she pushed up. She looked at them, seeing they were bruised where she'd fallen on them. Feigning more innocence than she felt, she said, "What's happening? What was that smoke? Did you...?"

"How did you break out of transport sleep? I have a high tolerance and so my transport always emits a higher dose." He glanced over her naked body. His eyes stayed on her breasts a second longer than the rest of her. Feeling exposed, she tugged on her clothing. The shoulder was ripped and she was forced to tuck it in to hide the tear. It was much easier for him to right his clothing as he pulled his waistband up over his cock and pushed the facility uniform around his thighs. "I don't know how you are used to doing things on your plane, but normally there is a mutual understanding before sex."

"Mutual..." Her mouth dropped open. "Hey, *you* drugged *me*. On my plane we have forms to sign before sex can commence. I didn't consent to coitus *or* being drugged."

"I vaguely recall your head being in my lap."

"I didn't put it there," she defended. "I fell. That's not my fault. You drugged me." She rubbed her neck. "I asked you what you were giving me. You should have said it would have an arousal side effect."

"You didn't fall into my pants."

"You didn't fall into my pussy." She arched a

brow, irritated beyond reason. The transport made another hissing noise. A mist entered. She lifted her hand. "Oh, no, you don't get to drug me again to try to get out of this."

"Relax. It's to help us wake up." He frowned at her. "We must be at the biosphacility."

Her head did begin to clear as the mist surrounded her. She swept her hands over her hair, smoothing it. As if by mutual agreement, they changed the subject. "Biosphacility?"

"It's short for Biosphere Facility. We call this location Biosphacility Three. This is the facility where Dr. Markos is assigned to work. It's one of the largest biosphacilities on the planet, and the most luxurious of our research bases. I am sure you will be comfortable, Sans Nel."

"Is there a medical library?" she asked.

"A computer will have access to any of the public records your boss requires." He frowned. "You forgot your parchments back at the hospital. I'll have someone scan them and notify you when it's complete. You should have access to it in a few days at most, probably sooner."

Linnea didn't respond to the veiled insult. What should have been a relaxing aftermath of great sex turned into a stiffly awkward conversation. Outside, fat trees opened up into a narrow ravine. Workers in full white containment suits kneeled around something on the forest floor. They were surrounded by green and purple plant life. "What's wrong with the air?"

He frowned, leaning forward to look at what she saw. "The air?"

Linnea pulled slightly away, not wanting to be too close to him now. "They wear suits. Has there been an outbreak of some kind?"

"It's protocol. There are pollens in the forest and any number of things that can create an allergic reaction." They watched one of the workers place a plant sample in a specimen jar. "They're testing the forest plants for genetic mutations."

The transport turned and Sam sat back in his seat. She continued to look out the window, very aware of where he was. She felt his eyes on her but she didn't meet his gaze. The biosphacility was a large dome, curving high off the ground. Tall gates encircled the stone encampment, keeping the forest separated from the inside. Covered walkways snaked out from the center facility like tentacles toward the gates, blocked by sealed doors to keep out the surrounding forest. The security gates were constructed of a ring of solid stone topped by several rows of thick metal bars. The closer they arrived, the taller the gates seemed until she could no longer see inside, her view blocked by the wall.

The transport stopped and made a series of fast beeps. The gate slid open just enough to let them slip through the wall. For a moment the transport became dark as they moved into the biosphacility.

"Won't the pollen get into the air supply anyway?" She glanced upward meaningfully, though she couldn't see the top of the security gate from where they were.

"The bars create a magnetic field that will keep out most pollens and any flying creatures. The thick wall keeps out other forest creatures that might otherwise cause allergic reactions in the staff. Sterilization protocols deals with any residual pollens and things we can't see." He paused in thought. "Once your boss learns our protocols, I'm sure she'll teach you whichever she deems necessary for your job. There is no reason for you to worry. The doctors have everything well in hand. You will be safe."

Linnea arched a brow. "Cecilia is not my boss. I am an inter-dimensional dignitary and merely here to assist." She was well aware she was making herself sound more qualified than she was. Well, she didn't have to tell him this was her first, and probably only, dignitary mission.

"My apologies." Though he said the words, he didn't sound apologetic.

"I might not have your doctor title, but I do have a brain." Linnea crossed her arms over her chest and sat back. She kept her eyes forward and didn't look out the window until the transport came to a full stop. Not for the first time she wondered what would happen to her. Would her plane abandon her here? Was this some elaborate plan to get rid of her, permanently?

She took a deep breath, refusing to give in to fear. If she kept her mind open, learned everything she could, more than Cecilia, her plane would have to take her back. She would know too much. If Sam couldn't cure her, then that was her next best bet—to be smarter and better than her traveling companion.

"Shouldn't be too hard," she mumbled.

"Excuse me?" He straightened his shoulders and quickly drew his hips back, clearly thinking she was talking about his arousal.

"Nothing." Linnea tried not to laugh as he adjusted himself on the seat. Dr. Arrogant might not like it, but it would seem he was still attracted to her and this time he couldn't blame it on being drugged.

The transport stopped and the door automatically slid open. Sam stepped out and held a hand out to help her down. Linnea gave him a knowing smile when she touched him, letting her fingers linger a little too long. He held his breath. Her smile widened. Good. Let him be uncomfortable.

Though, the way her body responded to him, this attempt at mischief might backfire.

The ground was covered with loose stones. Behind her, the transport door shut and the vehicle navigated itself to a parking spot in the biosphacility gate.

"I know you have a brain," Sam said, belatedly responding to her comment. "I saw your scans."

"Then do you think you can try talking to me like you do your doctor friends?" Linnea knew she should tread a little more gingerly with the Director of Central Hospital, but there was something about this frustrating man. She wanted him to know she was smart and not just some whore who pleasured men in power.

"Follow me, Sans Nel." Sam walked stiffly head of her.

"Yes, Dr. Swift." She mimicked his arrogantly cold tone. After a lifetime of defiance, she couldn't help herself.

The dome shone a little too brightly as the sunlight reflected off the shiny white plates of the exterior walls. Inside, he led her through a wide metal corridor lined with doors. She was beginning to sense an architectural theme on the planet.

"This is section one. This is where you will assist your boss, excuse me, Dr. Markos, in her work. The wall monitors, as well as the handheld device we supply you with, will have access to the public records as well as your papers once they're scanned. A laboratory with standard samples has been provided for the doctor's work. Again, she will be able to tell you how to work anything she needs you to assist with."

Because I'm clearly an idiot who can't figure it out for myself, she thought resentfully.

He paused briefly as they passed a door. "This will be your assigned laboratory." He didn't bother to take her inside. "This way to your private quarters. Narrow halls are for private areas. Wider halls are for general use. I recommend staying out of private halls you don't belong in as a courtesy to others."

Did the man even realize how insulting he sounded? What? Was she going to go raid the doctors' belongings? Snoop in their rooms? Streak naked in an ancient act of chaos?

"Dr. Fauchet took care of the luggage. If it's not here, it will be soon." Sam went into a room and gave a sweeping gesture. "This is where you will stay. Press the green button on the monitor if you need help, or basic instructions on how to use anything."

The smooth walls of the chamber were bare and lacked personality of any kind. This was one of their most comfortable facilities? There was nothing special about it that would set it apart from any other room on dimensional plane 187. A thick mattress with silver covers had been placed on the platform in the middle of the room. A health monitor had turned on with the lights. There was a small area for personal needs, a row of drawers built into the wall, and every basic necessity she should need. Her black luggage was already on the bed.

"I will let Dr. Fauchet know you have arrived. Someone will be by to take care of your daily sustenance. I hope my explanations have satisfied your request that I interact with you as I would any visiting doctor."

Linnea opened her mouth to answer, but he was gone before she could even so much as get out a thank you. "Way to pick a charmer," she mumbled to herself as the door slid shut. Even now, she wanted to seduce him. Pride kept her from even considering going after him. Instead, determined to get started learning, she opened drawers and poked around inside them. Only after she'd touched every strange, foreign object in the place did she turn to the monitor. "Okay, medical world, let's learn what you know."

8

LINNEA WAS EXHAUSTED, but she wouldn't let that stop her. She needed every ounce of time to learn what she could from this medical plane. They made it very clear that all medical documents were not to leave the plane unless pre-negotiated between the Medical Supreme and her home world's politicians. Linnea doubted her governing politicians would care about negotiating documents for her reading enjoyment back home. They tended to prefer arresting her for trying to check out medical books from the library.

Actually, the information was quite fascinating. It had taken her a week to figure out their work methods, but after that it became easier to navigate their public records. Since she was used to learning on her own, she had an advantage over her traveling companion. Cecilia seemed to struggle with the work. Granted, it wasn't easy to learn what equated to a foreign medical language, but Linnea was doing it.

"It's like reading an ancient medical cipher," Cecilia mumbled at the other side of the laboratory. The lab was large and they were the only two working in it. There were work tables, dozens of items of medical testing equipment, sterile tubes lining one of the walls. Though different in design, it functioned much like the technology on their home plane did—only more advanced. In the corner there was a sleeping cot. For the first couple of weeks no one had used it, then Linnea began to notice body imprints in the material—right after Dr. Fauchet had returned from wherever he'd been. Cecilia tried to act as if nothing was going on, but Linnea wasn't naive.

Seeing Cecilia frown at an electronic clipboard and rub her temples, Linnea thought about offering to help. The woman looked up at her with the superior expression of disdain she often carried. Never mind, let the smart doctor figure out for herself that she was painstakingly reading the cure for Policompition Ten. On their plane they called it Firghelm

Syndrome, a fancy name for itchy feet, and they'd cured it a lifetime ago.

Linnea chuckled to herself. She'd scanned over the same document their second week there. It was how she figured out that first translating the chemical formulas at the end of the document saved a lot of headache and time.

"Levels," Cecilia mumbled to herself. Linnea again considered helping the woman out with her translations, but realized the doctor would probably mock any attempt Linnea made.

The wall monitor dinged, indicating that Cecilia needed to take something to relax. It did that a lot. Apparently the woman was a giant ball of uptight.

"Can you shut that off?" Cecilia's tone was more of an order than a question.

Linnea looked up from her handheld, irritated to have her study interrupted yet again to do Dr. Markos's bidding. The other day the woman actually sent her to fetch food. Going to the wall monitor, she punched in a dismissal code to get the unit to stop beeping. If she wanted, she could have overridden the shot code. She'd discovered how to do so on accident in one of her readings. Instead, she left it. The monitors were set up to issue corrective shots whenever someone's emotional or physical levels strayed away from normal. It was designed for promoting an optimal work output. Cecilia was given a lot of shots. Linnea dismissed most of her personal ones, marking them as complete. The only shot she took was to correct her natural magnetism with the prescription Sam gave her.

"Our time here is nearly half over and all I've really learned is this plane is obsessed with immortality," Cecilia said.

Linnea knew from experience the woman wasn't really talking to her. There were numerous references in the public records relating to the pursuit of escaping death. Some tried to find the path to ascension, electrocuting themselves in the process, the rest of them just tried to cure everything and block out what they couldn't cure.

"Over half," Linnea corrected to get the woman to stop mumbling to herself.

"Half of what?" the doctor asked.

"You were mumbling out loud again," Linnea said, not glancing up from her work. "You said we were almost halfway done. In fact, we are over halfway done. As of yesterday, we are starting month two."

"It's this place. With no daylight it's impossible to keep track of the hours." Cecilia studied her.

"Go up to the top level. There's plenty of sunlight."

"The top level?"

"Haven't you wandered around at all?" Linnea asked, surprised. She'd explored most of the facility in the first week and talked with many of the staff.

"No. I've only gone where instructed, as should you. They showed us our quarters, the dining hall and our laboratory."

"Not surprising this," Linnea drawled. So much for friendly conversation. "You're one of those true believers in the anti-chaos, aren't you? One of the devout."

"No," the woman denied, obviously not liking the comparison to being a monk.

"Really?" Linnea was tired of being treated like some kind of imbecilic responsibility. She wasn't an idiot. She saw a lot more than Cecilia realized. "Then why all the shame about Dr. Fauchet?"

Cecilia stiffened. "I don't know what you mean."

"All right then." Linnea couldn't help herself. "It's about time for you to kick me out for your..." The woman paused, giving her a meaningful look. "Your nightly, serious, platonic, anti-chaos discussions with Dr. Fauchet."

Cecilia glared at her. "My professional medical

conversations with Dr. Fauchet, our inter-dimensional contact, are not of your concern. You haven't been to medical school so I understand that you have no idea the level of complicated maneuvering and paperwork involved in a mission such as ours."

Linnea set down her electronic clipboard and moved toward the door. If she didn't get away from the woman, she would do something she'd regret. Doing her best to look nonchalant, even though inside she churned with anger, she said, "A little hint, doctor." She ran her hand over the wall unit and smiled. "As you've pointed out on many occasions, I'm not a doctor, but in my experience, anti-chaos conversations work much better if you keep your clothes on."

Linnea left the woman gawking after her. Good. Let the superior doctor fret about just how much Linnea knew. It wasn't like she'd spread the gossip of it on their home plane, and no one on this plane cared about sexual affairs, but Cecilia didn't need to be told that. Let her worry about it. Maybe then the woman would treat her assistant with a bit more respect.

Thinking of sexual affairs caused her thoughts to naturally turn toward her own last encounter, Dr. Sam Swift. She hadn't seen him since he'd dropped her off, and she had no indication that she would ever see him again, but still she hoped. Her body ached for release, to be touched. She fingered the prescription necklace he'd given her. There were other opportunities at the facility, other doctors, some of them not bad to look at, yet she couldn't get Swift out of her mind. What she thought was a rude tour of the biosphacility turned out to be his way of treating other doctors. He might not always react when she spoke, but he had listened.

As she strode to the end of the corridor, she frowned, realizing she'd left her clipboard in the laboratory. There went her evening reading. She wasn't going to go back to retrieve it, not after the grandiose exit she'd just made. Deciding she didn't want to go to her quarters, she instead turned to go to the top of the dome. It was hard to tell time inside the base of the facility with its artificial lighting, but she estimated it to be evening by the subtle ways the lights dimmed in the narrow residential corridors.

"Dr. Lu will remain in Asclepius to oversee matters there."

Linnea stopped walking. The voice hit her like a shockwave. Sam was there, at the facility, and she hadn't known. Part of her was hurt that he would avoid her. The other part of her was all too willing to forgive him if he'd agree to fuck her again. She tried to push that primal part of herself down.

"I've commissioned Dr. Jonns to work on the problem like you asked, but I just gave him a piece of it and enacted Privacy Code Six. I don't trust him with secrets of this magnitude. He has been tasked with analyzing..." Dr. Gerard Fauchet's answer became muffled. Linnea couldn't be sure, but thought he mentioned some kind of virus. "...Sebastjan's new wife."

"Jonns is a capable doctor, but I agree," Sam said. "And our guests? Do they suspect anything?"

"No. Nothing. They spend all their time in the laboratory. Dr. Markos has had her assistant access several medical documents, more so than what shows up on her personal records, but I don't think she's trying to steal them. I think she might have trained Sans Nel to scan them for possible coding. If we weren't so busy, I'd have analyzed their scroll patterns."

"We'll order the dignitaries checked when the time comes for them to leave, *if* they leave. We don't need another Plane 33 incident on top of everything else," Sam said.

"I've integrated myself with Dr. Markos," Gerard

said. "Do you want me to have one of the others speak to Sans Nel?"

There was a long pause. "No. I'll do it. We struck up a rapport in the transport. The less who know of what we are about, the better."

Linnea frowned. A rapport? Is that how he remembered it?

"I'm supposed to meet Dr. Markos in a half hour. I'll offer to extend their stay for learning purposes."

"Good idea. No one ever refuses that offer."

Linnea heard footsteps and hurried back away from the door. She barely made it around a corner as she saw the hint of a lab coat peek from behind the office doorframe. Only too late did she realize she'd ducked into a residential hall and there was nowhere to go. She pressed herself into a doorframe and waited. Unless someone looked directly at her, they might not notice her there. She watched, listening as footsteps drew nearer. Gerard passed by, heading toward their laboratory with a syringe in hand.

As much as she didn't like Cecilia, she couldn't abandon the woman in light of what she'd just heard. She made a move to go after him.

"Sans Nel."

Linnea stiffened. She hadn't heard Sam's footsteps

behind Gerard's. She quickly turned. When she looked up at him she didn't want to believe him capable of deceit. Her mind froze and all reasonable thoughts left her. Desire instantly rose inside her, but she fought it, knowing she had to keep her wits about her. This plane had secrets and she needed to find out what those were. Her very future might depend upon it.

9

"WHAT ARE you doing in my hall?" Sam asked the woman before him. He had not planned on seeking Linnea out so soon after his arrival, but that didn't mean he hadn't wanted to. In fact, he'd wanted to turn his transport around the second he stepped into it a month ago. Duty had called him away, but his body had begged him to stay. Duty won, as it always would, as it had to. Too much was at stake.

When Gerard mentioned someone else questioning her, he should have allowed it. They wouldn't be the first dignitaries who tried to sneak recordings of documents back with them. That was the least of his worries. What he didn't tell Gerard was that he had other orders. With Privacy Code Six, he only revealed that which Gerard needed to do his job.

Sam's orders came from the Medical Supreme. Well, not directly, but they were clear. A strange outbreak had been discovered in the city that started the same time the two dignitaries arrived. There was no proof, but the coincidence couldn't be ignored. The alarm hadn't been a mistake. Not even the Medical Supreme could hide the virus report.

Linnea shot him a coy smile. Every thought slipped out of his head. Her tone lowered seductively, as she said, "I heard you were back."

"Oh?" That surprised him. "Did you require my assistance? How may I help you? Is it your prescription?"

She glanced down the hall both ways before again eyeing him. Her smile widened. "Transport ride."

At that he shook his head in denial. "I'm sorry. Now is not a good time to arrange trips."

Her smile didn't falter. She stepped closer and lowered her voice meaningfully. "Or perhaps just a ride?"

"Oh," Sam said, only get her meaning seconds later. "Oh, you meant..."

"For a smart guy you're a little..." She chuckled to herself. "Never mind, Doc. You have a good night."

"Wait." Sam reached for her arm, not sure what

to think about her offer or his sudden decision to take her up on it. "I apologize. It has been a very long month."

"I believe both of our months were the exact same length of time."

Sam wasn't sure if she was making a joke so he refrained from responding. Her smile dropped by small degrees. It was a subtle shift in her expression, but he caught it. In that moment, he had the feeling he couldn't fully trust her. And in that moment he wanted her even more.

"Are you upset with me?" Sam didn't let go of her arm, but instead began caressing the length of it.

Linnea trembled. "Why would I be upset with you?"

"For not contacting you after what happened in the transport." The second he said it, he saw her amusement and wished he could take it back.

"Well, according to my plane's customs, we are married now." She lifted her hand and stroked his cheek. "We did come together without consent forms. It is the law."

"Ah, I—" Marriage? A strange feeling began to unfurl inside him at her words.

Linnea burst into laughter. "Relax. We're not married. I'm teasing you. You're so serious."

"Of course." He dropped her arm. "I thought we were acting like doctors toward each other. I didn't expect the light comment."

"Forget I said anything about that. I was tired from the trip and I get grouchy when I first wake up." She dropped her hand from his face to his chest. "Show me this room of yours."

Sam didn't understand this woman. She teased him. She dismissed him. She had no regard for his high position of power. She wasn't afraid of him and she didn't seem to want anything from him personally.

Her hand slipped down to his hips.

Perhaps that last statement wasn't true. She did seem to want something very personal from him.

"My quarters." He gestured to his door.

"After you." She stepped aside to give him access to open the door. He waved his hand over the biometric scanner and led the way inside.

Linnea knew she could have walked away from Sam and he would not have followed her. She didn't trust him. She didn't trust his plane or his politicians. It was actually quite arousing, the mistrust, the suspicion. His very attitude brought out the rebel in her. His very nearness made her want to seduce him. Linnea smiled to herself. She always did have a problem with authority.

She had expected Sam's room to be bigger than hers, but in fact it was almost exactly the same. The only difference was the monitor on the wall. It was much bigger and appeared to have a lot more functions, including a small button in the corner marked "Privacy."

"Did you partake of your evening sustenance?" he asked.

Linnea reached for the hidden buttons fastening the uniform they'd given her to wear. She quickly undid them and let the material slide from her shoulders. His eyes instantly dropped to look at her body. The thin undershirt clung to her body, giving away the curves of her breasts and nipples. "No. You should probably feed me." She crossed to where he stood, took hold of his lab coat and pulled him toward the large bed in the center of the room.

He touched the prescription necklace he'd given her. "Has the treatment been working?"

Linnea nodded, the kindness in his voice causing her to falter a little. "Yes. Thank you. I've only needed two doses since that first."

"You've taken three?" He frowned. "The medicine should be lasting longer than that."

Linnea hid her emotions at the genuine concern in his eyes. She knew a cure was too good to be true, yet she'd dared to hope. Placing her hand over his, she urged his hand lower to cup her breast.

"Sam," she whispered, "I don't want to talk about my prescription. Either you'll find something to help me or you won't. Discussing it won't affect the outcome."

"You call me Sam," he said, as if surprised.

She pulled at his lab coat, tugging it open without unfastening the buttons. They gave under the force of strength. Leaning in to him, she kissed the center of his chest. "Doctor seems a little formal," she paused, kissing a few inches lower, "when," she kissed lower, "I'm about to..." Her words trailed off as she made her way to his waist. She tugged at his pants as she kissed his hip. He made a small moan of approval. His pants slid down his legs.

Linnea walked him around and then pushed his stomach so he sat on the bed. She explored his body, avoiding the towering arousal. His hips jerked whenever she rubbed her hands near his cock.

"Please," he begged, trembling at her touch. "Oh, *apolloa,* please."

Linnea smiled, liking that this powerful man succumbed so easily to her. She leaned over, letting her breath fall on the tip of his cock. His fingers threaded into her hair, but he didn't force her down, merely caressed her head. "I think it's about time I prescribed you something for this affliction."

"Yes, please, yes." He touched her breast, circling his thumb around her nipple.

She slipped a hand between his thighs, bracing her weight. The back of her wrist touched his balls. With her free hand she took hold of his cock, lightly gripping the smooth, firm shaft. "I think your temperature is elevated."

He groaned and stiffened.

"Let me see if I can bring this fever down." Linnea leaned over him and took the tip of his shaft into her mouth.

"I have never been with a woman like you, Linnea." The admission was more of a groan tinted with pleasure than actual words. "There is something special about you."

Linnea adjusted her positioning to take him deeper. She wrapped her hand around the base of his shaft, angling it to her mouth. He tensed, jerked, shivered, moaned for more. It didn't take long before he erupted between her lips. She pulled back and smiled at him. "I bet you say those sweet things to all your lovers."

"No," Sam breathed hard. He pushed up, maneuvering her body with his. "I don't keep other lovers."

The admission surprised her. "Surely a man in your position gets a lot of offers."

"I don't want to be used for my power." In one graceful motion he flipped her onto her back. Her body sank into the soft mattress.

Linnea let the playful mask slip from her face. She looked deep into his eyes, seeing the man he was within that gaze. "No one likes to be used or judged for what they are."

Sam kissed her, teasing her mouth with his. The light pressure sent little jolts of pleasure down her body. Her legs worked against him.

When he broke the kiss, he told her, "I have no reason to use you, and any judgment of you is favorable." Forcefully, he pushed apart her thighs. Gone was the submissive man from moments before.

She crawled up on the bed, moving away from him. He followed, again pushing apart her thighs. He looked up at her meaningfully as he lowered his mouth to her sex.

As his tongue tickled her clit with light, teasing

flicks, he drew her knee over his shoulder. Her calf pressed over his back. He held her leg in place, anchoring her pussy to his mouth. She gasped, finding it hard to breathe.

Linnea wiggled beneath him. His tongue worked along her slit before a finger found its way inside her body. He licked harder. She pushed up on the bed. Warmth centered on her pussy. She tried to speak and only ended up gasping his name over and over, "Sam, Sam..."

Sam stroked her deep, pressing two fingers into her. He sucked her clit. Pleasure built. Her toes curled. Her legs stiffened. She climaxed against his lips. Before the tremors subsided, he dropped her leg and pushed up between her thighs.

Sam's cock slid easily in the moisture created with her release. He groaned in pleasure. Her muscles stretched to accept him. He thrust deep before pulling out and thrusting again. His hips moved in small circles as he fucked her.

Linnea moaned his name. Sam rubbed her nipple. He kissed her neck, her chest. The pleasure coursed through her, making her forget herself.

The pace quickened. Tension built before erupting through her. Linnea tensed, coming again. Sam's body responded instantly as he came inside her. He froze above her, holding stiff as the pleasure washed over them. Then, falling to her side, he lay next to her.

"You should stay tonight." He touched her face, drawing her lips to his in a lazy caress. The soft movements were tender and sweet.

Linnea didn't answer. How could she? His mouth was on hers and she couldn't form a word to save her life.

10

LINNEA LOOKED at the man sleeping next to her. Sam's hand rested on her thigh. He'd asked her to stay, but when the kiss ended he hadn't cuddled her next to his body. Instead he stared at her questioningly in those moments before his eyes closed for the night. She didn't know what he silently wanted to know.

Linnea concentrated on his breathing for a long time, making sure he would not wake back up. When she was convinced he wouldn't wake up, she slid her leg out from under his hand. The light was dim and she saw more the impression of his features than his actual face. For a moment, she hesitated. Yesterday, she would have said this man was an arrogant doctor who treated her like every other person of power she'd ever met. Earlier today, she would have said he was a devious doctor with possible evil tendencies who was up to something shady along with the others on his plane. When he'd kissed her, she would have said there was no possible way this man was evil. Now, as he slept, so sweet and trusting, she didn't think him devious or arrogant. Had she been wrong about him? Or were her emotions getting in the way of her judgment?

It was wiser to mistrust him. Safer too.

Crossing naked to the wall monitor, she hit the setting to dim the screen. As she suspected, the unit had higher security access than the one in her room. She mouthed as she typed, "Privacy Code Six."

The unit brought up information on the code. Basically, it meant no one could discuss anything with anyone. She frowned, not finding the definition very helpful.

Next, she typed, "Plane 33 incident."

A long report appeared. She scanned over it to get the basic idea of what had happened. When Plane 33 visited on a mission similar to Linnea's, the doctors tried to steal copies of all of 187's records. That was bad enough, but they didn't stop there. They tried to transport some virus samples through the portal. Unfortunately, the viruses weren't completely secured for transport and they were accidently released on the other side. Plane 33 was nearly wiped out when the virus mutated. The population's immune systems weren't capable of fighting off the disease. Report notes at the bottom of the file indicated Plane 33 blamed 187 for releasing the virus as punishment for taking the medical records. Divinity Corporation acquitted Plane 187 from all wrongdoing and Plane 33 was sealed off permanently.

Two questions from her eavesdropping answered. But what did a privacy code and an old incident have to do with keeping them trapped on this plane?

Linnea glanced over her shoulder. Sam hadn't moved. She swallowed nervously before snooping deeper.

After a month of learning their system, she found her way through his files with minimal trouble. Only, when she tried to open the documents, the computer requested a bio-scan. She frowned, resetting the device as if she'd never touched it.

"What are you doing?" Sam's voice was sleepy.

Linnea stiffened and touched the necklace. "I can't sleep sometimes. I wanted to see if my prescription was wearing off." She turned and pasted a smile on her lips. "I didn't mean to wake you."

He didn't answer.

Linnea wondered how much he'd seen, but knew better than to confess before she was caught. "I should go."

"Stay."

"I should find food, uh, sustenance." She leaned over to pick up her lab coat.

"No, you should stay." He lifted his arm and waved her back into the bed. "The morning sustenance will be served in a few hours for the doctors who head out into the forest before dawn. It will be better than anything you can find now."

Linnea wasn't sure why she obeyed, but she did. She lay next to him and kissed him. He moaned lightly into her mouth and dropped his arm over her hip.

"I want to taste you again." Sam broke the kiss. His hand lazily skimmed over her thigh and butt. His eyes closed and he sighed heavily. The hand on her ass didn't stop its caresses. He made slow circles on her skin, rubbing deeper with each pass.

Linnea pressed her leg forward, placing her knee between his thighs. His hands roamed her body in sleepy caresses. Sam made love to her slowly, taking his time exploring her. His mouth kissed every inch of her flesh before finally settling between her thighs. She writhed against his tongue as he licked her pussy. He pulled her clit into his mouth and released it. When she was breathlessly begging for completion, he came over her to end their torment. He entered her steady and sure, pumping his hips until they found sweet release.

SAM WANTED TO TRUST LINNEA. When he looked deep into her beautiful purple eyes he sensed that he could. Holding her felt natural and right. Yet, when he closed his eyes, he was forced to remember his duty. Currently, the sick count was very low, but they didn't know how to cure the mystery virus. The idea frightened him. In his lifetime they had never seen a medical outbreak they didn't understand. There were diseases from other planes, but the similarities in biology combined with the collected knowledge from other realities only strengthened their medical confidence.

Linnea burrowed against his chest. He'd been hesitant to take this approach with her, but her teasing suggestions had been too much to resist. She wanted him and she boldly let him know as much. How could he refuse such an offer? After the thorough scan he'd given her on her arrival, he knew she wasn't a carrier of the new virus. He'd looked at her charts himself.

Nothing would be solved at this moment. His body was sated and relaxed for the first time in a month, actually much longer if he didn't count their brief encounter in the transport the day she arrived. He hadn't wanted his thoughts distracted by her, but he hadn't been able to stop thinking about her. Not even his former wife had made him feel this way.

Sam knew this moment wouldn't last. How could it? She would eventually go home. He would remain here. He was in charge of Central Hospital, a job that included overseeing countless projects.

"You can't sleep?" she asked, suppressing a yawn.

Sam realized he'd been stirring on the bed and must have awoken her. "I'm thinking about work. Go back to sleep."

She mumbled something incoherent and snuggled against him. He concentrated on her even breath before finally falling to sleep himself.

11

"Dr. Markos?" Linnea's stomach knotted in fear. Cecilia was gone. She'd waited for the woman in the laboratory, but when she didn't show up for work, Linnea had gone looking for her in her quarters. Cecilia wasn't there. She tried locating the doctor on the wall monitor to no avail. A brisk, panicked walk of the facility proved fruitless. The woman was nowhere to be found.

Linnea went back to the lab and started pacing. Cecilia wasn't the type to skip out on her duties. The woman didn't even leave the portion of the biosphacility they'd specifically told her she could go to. Something must have happened to her traveling companion.

Linnea grabbed a laser scalpel off the supply wall

and went back out into the hall to make her way toward the executive offices. She didn't really think about what she was doing. That seemed to be a problem she had lately. She'd slept with Sam and hadn't really thought out fully what she was doing. If Gerard had done something to Cecilia while she was busy sexing up the enemy, she would never forgive herself. She might not want to invite Cecilia over for drinks, but that didn't mean she wanted her harmed. She thought of the syringe Gerard had been carrying. At the time she assumed it was medicine. They were always injecting themselves with medicine to correct levels.

Luckily, when she woke up Sam had been gone and she didn't have to face him. Had she known he'd just leave her alone in his quarters, she would have waited until morning to search his wall monitor.

"Bedlam and anarchy, Cecilia, where are you?" she whispered.

She hid the scalpel behind her leg as she passed by a group of doctors. They were more interested in discussing the figures on their clipboards than looking at her. Still, she held her breath as she moved past them. What was she going to do? She was trapped here. The forest didn't look too scary. Maybe she could run away and they'd be too frightened of germs to come after her. But then what? She'd live in the forest eating twigs on an alternate plane of reality? How was that a good idea? And if she made it back to Central Hospital, then what? Even if she managed to find her way to the portal, she had no idea how to run it. She truly was at the mercy of plane 187.

Gerard's office was empty. Her hands shook and her heart pounded. She wasn't sure what was happening, but she didn't trust anyone on this plane.

"What am I going to do?" she whispered, staring a moment longer into Gerard's office. She continued to the next office, passing by when she saw Dr. Jonns on the inside. His back was to her as he transmitted a communication on the wall monitor. The image of another doctor shone back at him. Linnea couldn't hear what they were discussing from behind the thick glass wall separating the office from the hallway.

"Linnea?"

Linnea gripped the scalpel tighter and turned to Sam. His expression gave nothing away. The softness from the night before was gone, replaced by the serious expression he'd worn the day they met. He came closer.

"What are you doing here?" he asked.

Out of habit, she reacted to his authoritative tone and instantly gave a sarcastic answer, "What? Didn't you miss me, sweet one?"

He glanced around before taking her arm and ushering her inside an empty office. With a quick set of the wall controls, he dimmed the glass to give them privacy.

Before he could speak, she said, "Don't worry, Doctor, I'm not here for you. Dr. Markos is missing. You wouldn't happen to know anything about that, would you?"

"Missing?" His expression didn't change.

"Don't play innocent. I know something is going on here. I saw Dr. Fauchet going toward our lab last night with a syringe. What happened? Did she refuse your offer of an extended stay? She did, didn't she? Dr. Markos would never agree to an extension. Changes like that create chaos in the government schedule and Dr. Markos is all about maintaining order. So what? Did Dr. Fauchet do something to her because she didn't want to be here?"

"Do something to her?" he repeated before shaking his head. "Of course not. Dr. Fauchet arranged for her to leave the biosphacility."

"Without me?" She stiffened. Emotions welled inside her and she found it hard to hold them back. It had occurred to her at one point that her sister sent her to this new world to get rid of her. She'd never really believed they'd actually abandon her here. At least, she'd hoped not.

"Yes." The word was slow and confused.

What if he was lying? What if they'd done something to Cecilia? "I don't believe you. I know about Plane 33 and I know about the Privacy Code Six." She was probing, but he didn't have to know that.

"You know?" His blank expression filled with panic for the briefest of moments. "What did you do?"

She didn't know how to respond so she stayed quiet. Accusation was not the reaction she'd been expecting.

"Is this revenge for Plane 33?" He set his clipboard down a little too hard and took an aggressive step for her. "That wasn't our fault. They stole from us. I don't know what they told you but..."

Linnea stumbled back at his sudden moves and lifted the laser scalpel in warning. "Stay back. I know what's going on here. Your plan is to delay us. It won't work."

"Are they allies of yours? Is that why you infected the...?" He eyed her laser but didn't seem too concerned. He did, however, stay back. "Is this for revenge?"

"You're worried." Linnea lowered her arm. "There's a disease here that you don't know how to cure, isn't there? Someone important is sick and you're all scrambling around for an antidote. If you suspect us, it must be in your capital city and it must have started about the time we arrived. You started to say we infected *the*...so, who?" She frowned, studying him. "The Medical Supreme."

His tense expression and lack of denial was answer enough.

"I don't know what evidence you think you have, but we haven't done harm to anyone. We are what we say we are, dignitaries on a learning mission. That's it. If you're going to accuse us of being danger-ous, you best have evidence."

He glanced at her weapon.

"This is for protection." She dropped her arm and hid the scalpel behind her leg. "You've been lying to us."

"Lying? No. We simply have no reason to tell you everything. Privacy Code Six has been enacted."

"Then you will let us go home?"

"I'm sorry." He shook his head in denial. "That is not possible at this time. All portal travel has been suspended. We will not risk an outbreak spreading to other planes. I'd hoped Dr. Markos would have agreed to stay longer for research."

"Without full disclosure of the risks?" Linnea arched a brow. "Why would we want to stay when you have some kind of outbreak?"

"It's contained for the moment. You would not be put into any undue danger. It is actually safer we keep you away from the capitol. If you were a doctor, I would explain it to you, but—"

Her hard look cut him off. She gripped the scalpel, resisting the urge to throw it at him. She was tired of being treated like an idiot. Through tight lips, she said, "Try."

"It's very complicated—"

"Then try hard."

"Sans Nel." He sounded exasperated. "Perhaps you have misinterpreted our intimacy to mean you should be afforded certain privileges. I take full responsibility for the lack of communication prior to seducing you. So to explain now, however belatedly, our intimacy does not equal full disclosure of my job. Some things I cannot discuss with you. It is not to insult you, but frankly it is very complicated and I don't have time to teach you how to be a doctor."

Linnea had never wanted to cut someone so

badly in her life. "Oh? Did you drug me to make me have sex with you, powerful and great Dr. Swift?"

"Well, no, of course not." He looked insulted.

Good, he should be insulted, she thought, barely able to control her ire. "Then you're just an arrogant nit."

"I-I..."

"Make no mistake, Doctor, I seduced you. I'm not some helpless Sans who swoons at the very sight of your manly brain. And, to be honest, your records aren't all that hard to read. Our languages are similar enough, only your plane seems to like to name diseases after the doctors who discover them and mine likes to name them after dead politicians and anti-chaos heroes."

"So Dr. Markos taught you to read the medical documents?" he asked. "Dr. Fauchet mentioned she has had you access more of the records in the short time you've been here than most dignitaries do in most trips."

"Seriously?" Unable to help it, she gave a small laugh.

"What is so amusing?"

"Dr. Markos is a highly respected medical mind on our plane, but that doesn't automatically qualify her to understand everything you do here. Her traditional training may work against her in that regard. She's used to things being a certain way. I, however, am self-taught, so my method of learning tends to be less rigid than hers." Linnea felt as if she might be bragging, but she really wanted him to stop looking at her like she was some stupid Sans. "I accessed your documents for my own use. Dr. Markos has me logging notes and running errands."

"*You* read all those documents?" To his credit he didn't look totally shocked and insulting as he said it.

"I scanned most of them. Once I convert the charts over it's pretty easy to see if what I'm reading is comparable to what we know of on our plane. If it is, I move on. If it's not, I spend the time studying it." She waited for his laughter. It didn't come. "I actually find it fascinating."

"If this is true, then why are you not a doctor?"

Linnea touched the purple stone at her neck. "Because of this. My anti-chaos chip doesn't work because my body rejects them. For this reason I was not allowed to continue my education beyond the basic required levels. This is the closest they'll let me get to medicine, assisting Dr. Markos."

"I won't pretend to understand the logic of refusing education to someone with a natural talent for it." Sam sighed. "My apologies for assuming you would not understand."

It was the first time someone actually, genuinely apologized to her since she was a child. She nodded, unable to speak as emotion choked her. Linnea set the scalpel on the desk.

"If you know of Privacy Code Six, can I take your word you will not discuss what I'm about to tell you?" He waited for her nod. "Good. This is not being made public. We would have a worldwide panic on our hands if people found out. This is no outbreak. The illness is contained for the time being. That alarm you heard when you arrived was the first indication of it. I have spent the last month ensuring a full sanitation of the hospital, transports, and the homes of anyone who could have come in contact with it. We've also isolated a way to detect the virus into the medical scans. We know you are not a carrier. We do not know why someone might be immune."

"How many?"

"At this time, one."

"Only one? So I was right? It's the Medical Supreme?"

"That cannot be known," Sam insisted. "Please, don't speak of it."

She nodded.

"I discussed the situation with Dr. Lu, whom you met when you arrived. We determined to authorize Dr. Markos, and this was before you told me of your knowledge, that if necessary we would allow her to work on the problem. Gerard vouched for her. Since you have clearly deduced the situation, I will allow you the same courtesy. We are not too proud as to refuse help. Our hope is that we can keep this incident contained. The Medical Supreme will not be pleased when he finds out about your involvement. If you agree, I cannot guarantee he might not institute consequences."

"Is that where you took Cecilia? To work on this?"

"No, Gerard took her out of the biosphacility. He thought she could use the break. Our logs show she's spent almost every hour between the laboratory and her quarters."

Linnea glanced toward the door. "So, you track where people go?"

He gave a small laugh. She quickly turned her attention back to him at the sound. "You like to wander."

"I call it exploring my environment."

Sam lifted his hand to touch her face. He looked

as if he wanted to kiss her, but he held back. "I will have a private file sent to your clipboard. Use LinSanNel as an access code to open it."

Linnea stepped closer to him. With his easy acceptance of her intelligence, and his willingness to believe her without real proof, she found herself even more drawn to him. There had always been a connection between them, a strong physical pull, but this was different. She felt...well, honestly, she wasn't sure what she was feeling.

"Maybe you should send it to your room?" Her eyes dipped to his mouth, giving meaning to the words.

His breath caught. "I would like nothing more than to take you back to my quarters, but I have another conference scheduled with Dr. Lu."

"Perhaps later?" She arched a brow playfully.

Sam appeared torn. "I, ah, yes. We should...later."

Linnea pushed up on her toes and pressed her lips to his. Her hand went to his waist. "Or maybe we should now?"

It didn't take much convincing to get his pants around his ankles. There was one advantage to wearing multiple pieces of clothing compared to the one full suit common on her plane—better access. No doubt that is how the fashion of the single-piece jumpsuit evolved, to keep anything chaotic and fun from happening. She unfastened her pants before reaching for his cock. She stroked the hard shaft, which didn't need much provocation to find its full length. He backed her into the desk and lifted her ass so she sat on the edge. Coming between her thighs, he thrust in. He took her almost desperately, burying himself in her depths. The angle of their lovemaking forced her to fall back on her elbows. He held her thighs, rocking her body back and forth to keep rhythm with his hips. Her knees were enveloped by the length of his lab coat. Oh, but it was rough and hard and felt so good.

As the tension built, she stiffened. He kept moving as he watched her come. Tremors racked her with endless waves of pleasure. Only when they began to lessen did he allow himself to join her. He buried himself deep, jerking violently as he came. When he finally let her go, the sticky feel of his seed wet her thighs.

"I could keep you in here all day for that." His breath was labored as he righted his clothing.

"And miss your meeting?" She shook her head. "You just be sure to find me when you get a break later."

Dr. Lu's image flashed on Sam's monitor, indicating a call. The man was late for their meeting, but considering Sam needed a few minutes to right his clothing and smooth back his hair after his surprise encounter with Linnea, he was grateful for it. Just thinking of the woman caused him to take a deep breath before he could accept the call.

Dr. Lu wore a frown when the connection established. Without preamble, he said, "I just spoke with Dimensional Plane 303's politicians. Politician Shinclus emphatically explained on behalf of his people that they are not happy with the change in plans. He's threatened to inform Divinity Corporation if their dignitary is not returned on schedule. The Medical Supreme neglected to inform us of an Anti-Chaos treaty he signed with them. If we neglect to return their doctor, they are entitled to unlimited medical access."

"Why would the Medical Supreme agree to such a thing?" Sam shook his head in frustration. "That makes no sense. What do we get out of the deal? We're the hosts."

Dr. Lu didn't readily answer.

"It's a secure line. Speak." Sam leaned closer, even though no one could hear them.

"New Order Society made him a personal trade," Dr. Lu finally answered.

"Which is...?"

"Sans Nel. Apparently, she has something biological wrong with her that isn't dangerous, but that makes her incompatible with the technology on her plane. The New Order Society government of their plane gave her to the Medical Supreme as a ward. It is unclear if she knows about the arrangement." Lu averted his eyes. "I managed to read the copy Politician Shinclus was only too happy to supply. He already indicated that he expects a full list of all of our plane's technology and that is just to start."

"A ward?" Sam froze. He wasn't an idiot. He

knew exactly what being a ward of Supreme Walter entailed.

"We have no choice. We have to send the doctor back in four weeks."

Sam shook his head. "We can't risk that this virus might mutate. The health risk later will be much greater than it is now."

"The Anti-Chaos treaty says nothing about sending her home early. Two weeks should be enough to confirm it's safe to use the portal if we follow all of the stringent protocols. I would bring them back here for the testing though, in case we need to send them home sooner." Lu shook his head. His eyes said more than his mouth ever would. He was not a fan of the Medical Supreme, though he had yet to vocalize an opinion on the man. Sam couldn't fault him for that. To speak out against the highest power on their planet was to commit career suicide. The Medical Supreme controlled everything. "I am handling Politician Shinclus for the time being, diplomatically. However, he continues to send demands."

"We should not have been put into this position," Sam grumbled under his breath.

"We have to show 303 we're in control," Lu insisted.

"I agree. Two weeks." Sam found the words hard to say. He didn't want to lose Linnea. The thought of her belonging to the Medical Supreme was intolerable. "But we're sending them both back. It will be a way to show them we do not need anything from them."

"Are you sure?" Lu's expression lightened some.

"Yes." Sam nodded. He knew the Medical Supreme wanted to trade for sexual wards. He'd already tested Sam's position on it. Sam couldn't do it. He had a feeling Linnea had not been told about New Society's plan for her. "And let's not mention the ward trade. I don't think Sans Nel is aware of the arrangement and we don't need an incident."

Lu seemed only too happy to agree. "I'll get the Medical Supreme to sign off on sending the dignitary back. I'll make the request vague and I'll get him to sign off on it."

"After medication might be the best time."

Lu nodded in agreement. "Consider it a supreme order."

"We'll leave in the morning." Sam pushed a button to end the communication.

Two weeks. It didn't seem fair. He wouldn't be ready to send her away in two weeks. However, it was for the best. He couldn't allow her to become a ward of the Medical Supreme. Nothing about that surprised him. Linnea was beautiful and spirited. Any man would be lucky to possess her. Sam was the lucky one she chose. The Medical Supreme's last ward, Sans Ariella, had just married his son. The timing was suspicious considering the wedding was planned right before Linnea arrived. Though, he couldn't see Sebastjan Walter marrying his father's lover.

Sam pressed his hands to his temples briefly before automatically going to the monitor to get an injection. The unit beeped as he was reaching for the syringe. The medicine might ease the headache, but it would do nothing for the stress that caused it.

1 3

Linnea toyed with the food on her plate. She found the things she missed about her home plane were few, but flavorful food was definitely one of them. Here, every meal tasted the same, unflavored and lacking in vibrant colors. Half the time, the food was in paste form and wanted for texture.

"Is the substance not to your liking?"

Linnea smiled before she met Sam's gaze.

"Your records indicated you have lost mass." He sat across from her with a plate.

"The substance is," she looked down at the pale green paste, "substance."

He chuckled. "I have been told though incredibly healthy, our food lacks the flavors of other planes." He took a bite. "It tastes normal to me."

"That's almost sad," Linnea said.

"We used to have culinary doctors, before the full enforcement of medical contraband laws. Most of the old spices were deemed unnecessary and unhealthy. Synthetic nutrients are much more optimal."

"I suppose it comes down to what you want most —a long life, or a flavorful one." She pushed the plate away. "I looked at the records. I'd like a couple days before I give any opinions."

"Of course." He ate, not really chewing before he swallowed. She wondered what he'd think of the food on her plane. "We leave in the morning for Asclepius. Will you tell Dr. Markos?"

Linnea nodded. "Of course."

"We'll have access to more tools at Central Hospital, and it is closer to the portal." Sam quickly finished his food and pushed it aside. Like most people, he considered the meals merely necessary breaks, like taking a shot when the monitor required it. There was no pleasure in the experience. "Do you miss your home?"

Linnea thought about his question. "Some things, yes. Like the food. Some things, no."

"It's been determined that you will be permitted to go home early."

"How early?" She wasn't ready to leave. There was so much she could still learn.

"Two weeks." He studied her face.

"I would rather stay the full term of my mission."

"It is for the best. We'll follow the most stringent of our protocols to ensure the safety of your plane, but then you should go." Sam kept his eyes steadily on her, as if taking in every nuance of her expression.

"I think Dr. Markos will be pleased. I'm not sure why she agreed to come on this mission." Linnea knew she shouldn't be talking about her companion, but there was something about Sam that drew her honesty. "That is not to say she is not very capable, but..."

"It is a big step for anyone to be one of the first to come through a portal. I will not think less of her for missing her home plane." His hand slid over the top of the table to rest near hers without touching her.

"Will two weeks be long enough for you to cure me?" Linnea's gaze traced the lines of his tapering fingers. She reached her pinkie toward his hand, barely touching him. Doctors ate around them, but none of them seemed to care about one of their highest medical officers talking to a lowly Sans. "I know it's selfish to ask. If it's not possible, I understand. The lives of many are worth more than my convenience."

"I could make sure you have the medicine you need. Whenever you had to be around computers, you could take it." His fingers inched closer to her hand. His little finger slipped over the top of hers.

"Thank you, but the injections are becoming more frequent as you warned they would. I'm not sure how much good they would do on my home plane. I need a cure. We have implants that don't work in my body for some reason. I can't be tracked. This makes me a threat to society. Without monitoring, I will still not be able to go to school or work in the medical field." She tried to hide her disappointment. "But the health of many takes precedence."

A small smile curled on his lips. "You have the doctor's spirit. Your plane is foolish for not seeing it in you."

Linnea drew her hand from his and stood. She trembled with emotion, but tried not to let it show. He was the first to see it in her. The knowledge was bittersweet. The one person who saw her potential didn't exist on her world and she was being sent away from his. In two weeks she would be exactly who she was before—an anti-chaos criminal who had to sneak into the library to read and who went home alone to a two-room apartment in the cheapest part of town.

"Thank you." She nodded. "I'll go inform Dr. Markos of the plan."

Sam looked like he'd stop her, but she turned and left before he could speak. Linnea wasn't sure why she walked so fast once she was out of his sight. She found it hard to breathe. She wasn't ready to go home. When it came down to it, she would do what was right, would put other people before her needs, but she really wanted a cure. If this plane did anything, it taught her how badly she wanted to study medicine and do research. It was what she was born to do. She'd had a taste of it here, with the documents Sam entrusted to her.

And then there was Sam. She stopped by the laboratory door before entering and took a deep breath. Sam.

"If you could come with me..." Cecilia's voice from inside broke into her thoughts.

Linnea blinked, realizing tears were in her eyes. She quickly brushed the moisture away to hide the emotion.

"That's not...no medical database is...with what I know, it would never be allowed," Gerard answered.

Linnea leaned closer to better hear what they were saying. "We'll figure something out."

"It's not like we can send communications to each other or visit each other on work breaks," Cecilia said. "I told you from the beginning this couldn't go anywhere, that it couldn't mean anything. There will be this invisible wall between us, keeping us apart. We will spend our entire lives waiting on the whims of our politicians that I can someday come back."

"You would wait?" he asked.

"What do you think love is?" Cecilia responded, her voice rising. "You think I'll just go home through the portal and it will all go away?"

Linnea suddenly felt guilty. She shouldn't be listening to their private moment. Clearing her throat, she pushed open the door and stated, "Doctor."

Cecilia stiffened, startled by the intrusion. "What!"

Linnea stood in the doorway, uncomfortable. She averted her eyes. Gerard made no attempt to hide his emotions. The love he felt showed on his face.

"What is it?" Cecilia said, softer. The woman's expression was composed but she couldn't hide the truth of her feelings as they showed in her eyes.

Linnea slowly backed away. "Dr. Swift sent me to inform you we're leaving the facility in the morning."

"I didn't mean to yell at you." Cecilia looked helplessly at Gerard. "I'm overwhelmed at the moment."

"I understand." She nodded once. The second she was alone in the hall, she thought again of Sam. Would he ever look at her the way Gerard had been gazing at Cecilia?

Two weeks wasn't enough time.

14

Sam wasn't sure what he was expecting when he knocked for entrance into Linnea's quarters, but finding her sitting on the floor surrounded by electronic clipboards wasn't it. Her hair was twisted into strange knots at each side of her face, keeping the locks out of her eyes as she leaned over.

"I can't be sure, but..." She pointed at a clipboard to her left before looking up at him. "This thing looks like it's airborne, or at least mutated. Infected Subject One was infected, but no one seems to know how. A report just came in that two people on Infected Subject One's staff tested positive for the virus. I'm trying to determine the incubation period, but I can't find the earliest possible time the staff could have been exposed. I'm trying to access their work and travel records to see if they were with Infected Subject One prior to their staffing assignment."

"More are infected?" Sam hurried to look at what she was pointing at.

"The message just came in an hour ago," she said, looking almost guilty.

"How did you see this before me?" He picked up the clipboard and began scrolling through the file.

"I told you I have a knack for learning." Linnea stood. Her beautiful eyes searched his. "I read all the files and I wanted to make sure I had the most up-to-date information."

Sam wasn't sure if he was impressed or frightened by her talents. She'd broken some of their highest encryption keys.

When he didn't readily speak, she said, "It appears airborne. There was no direct contact, if the reports are to be believed. I've looked over your standard protocols and they're very detailed. Unless the Medical Supreme, I mean, unless Infected Subject One is intimate with his staff members, I doubt there is any other method of transmission."

"Not in quarantine. The computers would sense it if there were physical activities of that kind." Sam pushed a few of the clipboards over with his foot and sat next to where she had been on the floor. She rejoined him. "If these numbers are correct, the incubation period is short. That means it should be safe for you to go home. The Medical Supreme's staff was brought in for their specialties, so there was no prior exposure. If there were more infected, we would see more cases. Maybe it's contained?"

"I've been looking at something else. I don't have a formalized report, such as your plane seems to like, but..." She handed him one of the clipboards. "Does this look familiar to you?"

Sam eyed the virus. "Yes. It's the new—"

"No," Linnea interrupted. "It's not..." She pointed toward the far side of her layout. "Can you hand me that one?"

He obliged, but said, "Our databases were scanned. Nothing matched."

"I know I've seen something like this. When I first arrived I went through some of your older records. I stumbled my way into the archives." She handed him the clipboard with a sigh. "Can you bring up my viewing history? About a week after I arrived?"

Sam did, handing it back to her.

"I know I've seen this..." Linnea mumbled to herself as she worked, scrolling through documents. "Only it wasn't a virus. It was something..."

Sam watched her for a moment before picking up the new reports. This was not the evening he had planned, but he found he enjoyed sitting with her. She made adorable little noises when she read something she didn't like. His eyes strayed to her hair puffs. They revealed her delicate earlobes. He found himself leaning toward her neck, intent on kissing her.

"Here!" She gave a tiny jump and thrust the handheld to him. "It's a control substance of some sort. It seems to be a few mutations back, but do you see it?"

Sam took the document. She was right. The document was listed as a human control experiment, not as a disease, so it wouldn't have been logged and checked when the virus appeared. His stomach knotted. On principal he didn't like human control research. No person's will should be taken away. The thought reminded him of Linnea and how her plane traded her to the Medical Supreme. What was to stop them from trying to trade her through the portal again if he sent her back? He couldn't protect her if she wasn't with him. When he looked at her, he couldn't let her go. At least he had two weeks to convince her to stay.

"Sam?" Her tone was soft and questioning. "Why are you looking at me like that?"

"You're very..."

"Am I in trouble? Is it because I opened the document? I'm sorry. Sometimes when I'm working I get focused and I don't think of anything beyond the problem. And this is a big problem. It might be the only medical problem I'm ever allowed to work on, so I might have gotten a little too focused. I apologize. I never meant to—"

"Smart," he broke in. "You're very smart and beautiful and unique and special."

"Oh," she said in surprise. Her cheeks pinkened at his words.

"Human control was a fad science decades ago," he said. "I doubt anyone ever looks at these old documents."

"Maybe you just don't know that they do," she said carefully. At his arched brow, she added, "Look at the lead doctor on the document."

Sam gasped. "The Medical Supreme."

"He does seem to like control," Linnea offered. He could tell she was trying to be polite while still giving her opinion. "And he was the first one infected. Even with your protocols, laboratory accidents could happen."

Sam looked at the basic outline of information. It would require deeper reading. "If he was, that would explain why he didn't tell anyone what he was doing. He should have recognized his own work."

"This document is dated. It is possible he didn't remember," she tried diplomatically.

Sam shook his head, not believing it. "No. Men like the Medical Supreme *are* their work. He would have remembered."

"I didn't mean to cause trouble." She touched his arm and he felt a jolt through his nerves. "Sam, if you tell me, I'll forget I found this."

"Don't you dare! The pursuit of truth, no matter where it takes us, is paramount to a decent life." He put his hand over hers. "But, we do have to tread carefully. It is not wise to accuse the highest power on our plane without solid proof."

She nodded.

"It's late and we have a transport ride tomorrow." Sam stood, reaching to help her up. When she moved to pick up her mess he said, "Leave it."

Linnea let him pull her to her feet. She smiled up at him. He loved that smile. He loved the low, seductive sound of her voice even more. "I thought you liked transport sleep."

"After our last trip together? I'm thinking of

disengaging the sleep aid." He caressed her cheek. He loved her soft skin. He loved her eyes. He loved her smell.

"Mm." The sound was a purr that made him shiver.

Sam was not one to lie to himself. He might have neglected to fully realize the truth until that moment, but now it stared up at him. He loved her. Not even the former wife had made him feel like this woman did. "I was married, previously."

Linnea blinked in surprise. "All right?"

"I thought you should know. It seems like something a person in a relationship would need to know." He placed his hand on her shoulder. "It did not work out and we parted ways. It was a convenient marriage for both of us. I don't have contact with her."

Linnea nodded but didn't speak.

Sam knew he was being ineloquent, but still he continued. "I don't have children. I have work."

"Are we in a relationship?" she asked.

"Yes." He nodded. Then, a little insecure, he added, "Aren't we?"

"I..." She hesitated. His stomach tightened and he found himself gripping her shoulder. He let go of her. "I think...yes."

He inhaled deeply. "Good."

"Good," she repeated. "I have never been married and I don't have children. I like children, but..."

"But?"

"On my plane, with my unique condition, I will never be permitted to have a child. My sister, Jinna, resents me a little because my condition will make her permit hard to obtain as well."

"You have a sister?"

"Yes, Politician Nel. She sent me here." Linnea gave a small, humorless laugh. "My family has written me off because I can't be monitored. I've always been an embarrassment to them."

"They are fools." Sam brushed his lips against hers. She accepted his kiss with a light moan of approval.

Her fingers skimmed over his chest to his neck. She pulled him closer. Her body pressed to his, molding perfectly against his muscles. He loved the feel of her. He loved everything about her. How could her family, her plane, not see how wonderful she was? One look at her clipboard notes and he could see she was highly intelligent. She found a very important key to their problem.

Their clothes seemed to melt away. Flesh glided

against flesh. Sam lifted her and carried her to the bed. They made love slowly. Her delicate hands traced every inch of his body. He massaged her in return. Hard nipples beckoned his hands. Soft thighs called to his hips. Flicking tongues met and tangled in passion.

When he entered her, he felt complete. He was never one for flowery thoughts, but he imagined this was what destiny felt like, the perfect fitting of two people. Her natural responses were timed to his. The tremors started deep inside her, calling forth his own release. When they came in unison, there was nothing else in all the planes he wanted.

15

LINNEA STRETCHED ALONGSIDE SAM, suppressing a yawn. It was late, but her mind wouldn't shut off completely to let her rest. Sam's eyes opened at the movement. He didn't look as if he'd been sleeping much either.

"I should transmit our findings to the others," he said.

"The Medical Supreme won't like it." She rubbed her knee absently along his thigh, liking the texture of his naked skin.

"The document is in public records. I won't mention his name directly, but the others will see the truth for themselves. He won't be able to hide it." Sam pushed up from the bed. "You deserve the credit for your work. I'll call you Dignitary Nel, not Sans

Nel, and I'll sign off as the doctor on your work. Please don't be insulted. If I call you Sans, they might not take the finding as seriously."

"I understand." She nodded, liking the sound of Dignitary more than Sans anyway.

"You realize this is your first official medical breakthrough." Sam gave her a quick smile as he picked up her clipboard and began organizing her findings into a preliminary report.

"Probably the only," she whispered. Linnea was keenly aware this would never happen again. In a way she was grateful for the opportunity to do what she always wanted to do. However, she had a feeling she would spend the rest of her life thinking back to this moment, to this wonderful man, and would languish over what once was.

"What?" he asked, glancing up at her.

"Thank you," she said louder. "I said thank you."

He smiled at her. There was an ease to him when he looked at her. Had it always been there? Had seeing the way Gerard looked at Cecilia opened her eyes to Sam?

She watched him compile his information, only speaking to offer suggestions a handful of times. He took her ideas graciously, adding them to his own. When he finished, he said, "I think that should do it for an update. We can write up a more formalized report for the records over the next few weeks."

A few weeks. Her smile fell at the reminder. A few weeks were not enough time.

"I'm sorry, I didn't mean to assume you needed my—"

"Yes, of course we'll do the report," she interrupted. "I'm just sleepy."

"You're right. It's late. We should sleep before the morning substance." He sent the update to his colleagues before turning off the clipboard. "Now the work is done there is nothing else to be done tonight."

"I wouldn't say nothing," she answered coyly, rolling to straddle his waist as he lay down. "I can think of one more thing we can do tonight."

"I am at your service, Dignitary Nel," he answered, opening his arms to accept her lovemaking.

16

LINNEA HEFTED her luggage through the long halls toward the transport area. She hadn't expected to feel emotional about leaving, but her hands had trembled as she packed her belongings. It had been tempting to slide an electronic clipboard into her bags. She refrained. She wasn't a thief.

"Let me help you."

Linnea turned just as Sam reached to take her largest bag from her. She let him carry it as they fell into stride.

"Where were you this morning?" he asked.

"I needed to pack and I wanted to speak to Dr. Markos, but I couldn't find her." Linnea slowed as they passed her assigned laboratory.

"They are taking a transport ahead of us. You

should see her at Central Hospital." Sam stared ahead, not meeting her gaze. She wondered at it but said nothing.

"Did you hear something about the report?" Linnea wondered aloud.

"I spoke with Dr. Lu."

Linnea waited for him to say more, but he didn't. When they walked outside, the transport box was waiting for them. She glanced around, half expecting someone from the biosphacility to take the time to see her off. The fact no one was outside to watch them go seemed a bit sad to her.

Sam put her luggage into a compartment below the seats of the transport before helping her inside. Once they were alone and on their way, she smiled at him. "Did you receive news from Dr. Lu?"

Sam reached into his lab coat and pulled out a small device. He fingered it gingerly, following the curved edge with his thumb. "He informed me that our report was received."

Her smile fell. The outside wall of the biosphacility passed by the window. "Did I cause problems?"

"No. We told the truth of what we found." He finally looked at her. "The report was automatically sent to the Medical Supreme. He wasn't pleased by the viral comparison to his old work."

"You didn't lose your job, did you?" The light smoke of the sleep aid began filtering into the transport. Linnea covered her mouth. "I thought you were turning the sleep aid off."

Sam took the small device and stuck it in his nose. "I'm sorry, Linnea."

"Sorry?" Panicked, she stood. Sam was there, holding his arms out to catch her as the drugs took effect.

"I love you, Linnea, I'm sorry."

It was the last thing she heard before sleep overtook her.

17

"Sorry?" Linnea croaked as she fought to wake up. Her blurred vision slid over the top of the transport. "Sam? Sorry?"

She pushed herself up too quickly and fell to the side, only to land on the floor. Crawling to the door, she managed to look out the window. Gerard ushered Cecilia inside the front door of Central Hospital. Sam stood behind them, waving that they should hurry. Linnea slapped her hand against the window. Sam glanced back at her, but didn't come to her.

"Sam?" Her voice became stronger. By sheer will she managed to stumble out of the transport toward the front of the hospital. What was happening? Why were they leaving her behind? Was she sick?

The hospital doors opened at her presence to let

her inside. She heard footsteps and moved to follow them. Her shoulder hit the wall and she used the smooth metal to keep her body upright as she walked. The monitor screens fuzzed as she passed, reacting to her.

"I didn't get to say all I needed to."

Linnea followed Gerard's voice around a corner.

"You did what you had to," Sam said. "I'm under orders to lock down the portal. We should go."

Gerard's eyes met hers. "I thought you said Sans Nel missed the transport."

Linnea stopped walking.

Sam turned to her briefly. "I..."

She couldn't hear what they were saying so she forced herself forward.

"...you trapped Linnea?" Gerard suddenly struck out, pushing Sam in the chest. Sam fell back into the wall with a loud thud and didn't fight back.

"What is...?" Linnea's voice was weak.

"I love her!" Gerard yelled, interrupting her. "Look at me. We just sent the most vital part of who I am through that portal." He pointed at a nearby monitor to his readings. It dinged several times, demanding he take a shot to calm himself. "Look!"

Linnea stumbled closer. She felt dizzy. Her legs begged her to rest, to slide onto the floor and sleep.

"Then go. Take your chances. Go. Follow her. Just go. I'll say you were sent as a dignitary. I'll say it was to maintain peace." Sam reached for the wall and grabbed a clipboard. He handed it to Gerard along with a medical unit from his lab coat. "These will help ease your way with 303 politicians once you get there."

"I'll take Linnea," Gerard said, making a move to help the woman. Linnea began to shake her head in protest. What was happening?

Sam grabbed Gerard's arm to stop him. "No. That's the deal. She stays. She will be invaluable in helping stop this disease. Now go. They'll be watching to make sure this section is sealed. If I don't do it, they'll do it for me offsite."

"But..." Gerard frowned. He gave her a guilty look. "Thank you."

Linnea watched Gerard leave as she slid to the floor. Sam didn't look at her for a long moment. Instead, he stared at the monitor then the portal room door.

"Sam," she said, demanding he pay attention to her. When he looked at her, the guilt in his expression was palpable. She tried to make sense of what she'd seen. "What happened? Why did they leave me here?"

"This morning when Dr. Lu called, he informed me that the Medical Supreme was not pleased with our report. He was going to send an order to us as soon as we arrived that the portal was to be sealed shut indefinitely. Both you and Gerard indicated that Dr. Markos would never be happy here so we sent her home."

"She left me?"

"She didn't want to," Sam said.

"That's a lie. My sister probably arranged to have me abandoned here." A tear slipped over her cheek. Her eyelids were heavy.

Sam kneeled beside her. "You know?"

Linnea hadn't expected him to admit it. "I saw you. You sent Cecilia away. You told Dr. Fauchet to leave me."

"I can explain. Gerard loves her. I had to let him go."

"You drugged me. You kept me here." She pulled her arm away from him when he tried to touch her.

"I needed more time to talk to you." He tried again to touch her and she slapped at his hand.

"We had time in the transport." Linnea managed to stand, forcing her trembling muscles to hold her weight.

Sam reached for her only to draw his hand away.

He paced the width of the hall in agitation. "I couldn't risk you not listening to me. If you go home, I can't protect you."

"Protect me?" She frowned in confusion. "It's my home. There is nothing to protect me from."

"They traded you to be the Medical Supreme's personal ward, Linnea. Next time it might be to one of the gladiator planes, or the newly discovered Staria where the men are centuries behind our times and speak of nothing but war and weaponry. Who knows what those barbarians would do to you. I couldn't risk you telling me you wanted to go. If you said it, I couldn't keep you here."

"So you trapped me here instead without asking?" In a way his intentions were sweet, though terribly misguided. Then the full enormity of what he was saying struck her. "What do you mean they gave me to the Medical Supreme? Like a slave?"

"A ward," Sam corrected.

"What is a ward?"

"You belong to him and he..." Sam didn't need to explain. The truth of it was in his jealously possessive expression.

"Sex slave," Linnea concluded. "And you trapped me here? To that fate?" Then, tears falling harder now even as she tried to maintain her composure, she demanded, "And you can let the happen to me? I thought we...I thought you..."

"You can marry me," he blurted. "The Medical Supreme could not touch you."

"Marry?" Linnea's legs gave out and she slid down the wall in shock. The floor felt like it moved beneath her. "You?"

He hesitated but nodded. "Yes?"

Linnea moaned, passing out onto the floor.

Sᴀᴍ ɪɴꜱᴛᴀɴᴛʟʏ ᴄᴀᴜɢʜᴛ Linnea in his arms and lifted her off the floor. He was surprised she'd managed to stay conscious as long as she had. He'd been even more surprised to see she'd managed to make it out of the transport and into the hospital on her own. The dose he'd given her had been strong.

"Well done, Sam," he grumbled sarcastically to himself. When Dr. Lu told him to send the women home, he'd panicked. He needed the transport time to think and plan. He needed to find the right words to tell her what her plane had done to her, what his plane had agreed to. That kind of thing wasn't easy to say. All of his medical training hadn't prepared him for it.

He carried her to a private room and laid her down on the examination table. The transport sleep aid was still in her system and he needed to deactivate it. Getting the right prescription from the wall unit, he spritzed her face a few times until she blinked and looked up at him.

"I didn't mean to trap you," Sam said before she could say anything. He was afraid she'd demand to leave before he had a chance to tell her what he needed to. "You were already planning on staying for four more weeks. I thought that would give us time. I thought if I..." Sam dropped his eyes. "No. These are all excuses. I cannot stand the idea of losing you. I love you, Linnea. You are smart and talented and you deserve to be a doctor. But I don't want those to be the reasons you stay with me. I want you to stay with me because you love me. If you don't, I won't force you. I will override the portal block and send you home. If you don't want to go home, I'll send you wherever you do want to go. If you want to stay here, I'll do everything I can to protect you from the Medical Supreme. It was selfish of me to not give you the option, but I panicked. I can run this hospital, coordinate doctors and researchers from around the known planes, but I don't really know how to do this. I love you. I don't want you to leave me. I don't want you to be a ward of the Medical Supreme. I don't want you to—"

"Sam," she said sternly.

"Don't leave," he insisted. Sam held his breath, waiting for her answer and afraid he'd been too ineloquent in his explanation.

"Sam—"

"If you don't want to marry me, that's fine. At least stay until this problem is resolved. The Medical Supreme is in quarantine. He can't have you."

"Sam—"

"Please, Linnea, I'll give you whatever you—"

"Anarchy and chaos, Sam, stop talking!" she yelled.

He snapped his mouth shut.

She pushed up from the examination table. That's when he realized he'd been leaning over her, pleading into her face, trapping her with his body. He stepped back, clearing his throat as he smoothed his lab coat nervously. His hands shook. His brain told him to speak, to fill the silence, to get on his knees and beg her. He'd never felt this before, not about work, nor his former wife, nor anything.

Linnea took a deep breath and looked around the room. Then, very calmly, she studied him. "I love you, too, Sam."

"No, you can't leave, please..." His words trailed off. He couldn't move. "Did you...?"

"Sam, I love you. You have shown me more respect than anyone I have ever met. I'm not pleased that you decided to let me deep transport sleep instead of telling me what was happening, and if you ever, *ever*, do anything like that again, the Medical Supreme won't be the only man in quarantine." She gave a small smile to lighten the threat. "Is that clear?"

"I won't. I panicked. I—"

"Sam," she warned. He shut his mouth and nodded. "That's a good doctor. Now come over here and kiss me."

It was a command he'd easily follow. In fact, he was pretty sure he'd do anything she wanted. Happiness welled inside of him as their mouths met. Tongues merged and stroked with tender promise.

"Does this mean you'll marry me?" he asked against her lips?

"Only if you promise to keep kissing for the rest of our lives."

His answer came in the form of a deep moan as he pressed his future wife back onto the examination table to make love to her.

18

EPILOGUE

"So you're the little bird New Society sent for me." The Medical Supreme gave Linnea a long look, as if examining her body for flaws through the quarantine glass. The man was locked away, isolated in a private care center, and still he acted as if he controlled everything in his universe. "Now that my son has married my last ward, I have an opening in my home that I am eager to fill. Ariella was pretty, but she didn't do for me what you're going to do for me."

Linnea knew she was safe. Sam would never let anything happen to her, yet the lecherous way this man looked at her caused her skin to crawl and her stomach to tighten with nausea.

They were underneath a small square building at the edge of Asclepius. The place looked like an old medical storage warehouse with plain exterior walls, flat roof and nondescript stone walkway leading up to serviceable doors. Inside the warehouse were stacks of wooden crates marked as carrying old supplies that were no longer used by this plane—cloth masks, antique injectors, and empty medicine vials. Buried in this jungle of forgotten supplies was a single crate that hid the stairwell to the quarantine beneath. That was where she was now, hidden from the world above, in a place few people were permitted to know about. In the center of the large basement room the Medical Supreme sat on a bed surrounded by thick plastic walls. His ashen features were pulled tight, but his eyes were sharp and mean.

"Your government was right. They said I'd be very pleased if I agreed to let you stay as part of the arrangement." The Medical Supreme's words hurt. No, she didn't want to go home. She had everything she wanted on plane 187—a wonderful husband, a future as a doctor, a life. Her hand strayed to her stomach—and a family. He must have seen her irritated expression because the man laughed and explained, "They don't want you back, but don't worry. I don't mind if you can't use computers or imbedded chips. That's not what non-doctors like you are for, is it, Sans Nel? Women like you are made to be on your knees, subservient. Come on in here and be a good little bird. There are privileges to satisfying the most powerful man on the planet."

Linnea gagged a little at the offer. She studied him as she would a caged animal and said nothing.

"Wait until I'm free, little bird," he promised.

"I found out an interesting fact from Dr. Lu," Sam said to the Medical Supreme, joining her. "It appears you did know what caused this outbreak, because you designed it to trap Sans Ariella to this plane and force her to marry your son. Only, you didn't count on them falling in love, did you?"

"Love?" The Medical Supreme snorted. "Love is an illusion. My son needed to marry. How else are we to pass on the line of power?"

"Yours is not a hereditary title," Sam said.

"Tell that to my ancestors who have been passing it down," the Medical Supreme answered.

Linnea turned to see Ariella in the stairwell. They'd been waiting for the Medical Supreme's son and daughter-by-marriage to arrive.

"Feeling powerful in your gilded cage, Father?" Ariella asked.

"I told you, wife, it's called a quarantine laboratory," Sebastjan said.

Ariella chuckled. "A cage is a cage."

"Stop enjoying this so much," the Medical Supreme warned.

"You did it to yourself," Ariella countered. She looked at Linnea. "I heard what he said and am very glad that is not to be your fate."

"You have no say in her fate." The Medical Supreme glared at them.

"Neither do you," Sam said. "She decides her own fate." He placed his hand on her shoulder. "As my wife."

"Wife?" the Medical Supreme spat. "I did not give you permission to marry her."

"We didn't ask you," Sam said.

"They asked me," Sebastjan inserted.

"You?" the Medical Supreme frowned. "You have agreed to be my Medical Supreme Proxy?"

"I truly regret to inform you, Dr. Walter," Sebastjan said, though he hardly sounded upset, "that due to your incurable illness, it has been decided that you step down as Medical Supreme."

"You can't do that!" the now former Dr. Walter yelled. He hit his hand against the quarantine wall.

"It's been done. Your successor has been named," Ariella said, taking her husband's arm. "Just like you wanted."

"I knew you would take the title." Dr. Walter

actually looked a little pleased with his son. "I knew you would grab the power when the time came."

"I have my duty to my people," Sebastjan said. "First, I informed the people of what you did to my wife and why it was necessary for you to step down from your position. Second, I approved Sam and Linnea's marriage. And last, I approved a new program to allow off-plane dignitaries to leave 187. Dr. Fauchet bravely volunteered to go to 303. Sam as already visited the plane and secured the position with Politician Shinclus. He was most pleased to deal with someone other than you. They were having a hard time coming up with the number of virginal women you had demanded in return for medical supplies."

"Suppressed hormones cause chaos," Linnea explained. "Virginity really isn't encouraged when people come of age."

"Last?" Dr. Walter asked his son, his hands pressing so hard to the transparent wall they turned white.

"Well, I supposed that was technically second to last. My last duty before resigning my post to Sam's very capable hands was to appoint Dr. Lu the new Director of Central Hospital." Sebastjan smiled.

"You can't do that!" Dr. Walter slammed his

hands for emphasis. "That title of Medical Supreme belongs to our family!"

"I have told you before. I have no desire to be Medical Supreme," Sebastjan said. "The position requires fresh blood."

"It is your birthright," Dr. Walter interjected.

Linnea watched the scene play out with interest. She was proud to call Sebastjan and Ariella her new friends. Sebastjan was nothing like his father.

Sam's hand slipped around her waist and pulled her closer. "And my first duty was to appoint my new wife as the hospital coordinator. It was her hard work that discovered your virus's true origins as a human control agent. It turns out she has a real knack for organization."

"I gave them the mansion," Sebastjan said. "It does come with the job."

"That's mine!" Dr. Walter growled in frustration. "What are you going to do? Leave me here?"

"For a few months. Then you will be moved to a new quarantine facility being built in the country," Sam said. "There you will live the rest of your days with your two infected attendants. They've agreed to the arrangement, but do not mistake them for servants."

"It's your own fault." Ariella stepped to the wall

and faced him. She placed her hands opposite his on the barrier. "You have learned nothing from your mistakes. You are a miserable person. The goddesses have seen fit to punish you for it. You will live as you had me live, as a prisoner within your new home."

"Enough of your goddesses." The confined man snorted.

Sebastjan took his wife's arm and led her toward the stairs.

"Wait!" Dr. Walter yelled, almost desperate. Sebastjan looked at him. "You will come to visit me?"

Linnea almost felt sorry for the man. She did not know the former Medical Supreme as these people did, but he seemed almost broken in that moment. Sebastjan took pity on his father and nodded once before disappearing.

When the couple was gone, the man turned to Sam and Linnea. "What will become of me?"

"You will be allowed to work on curing this virus you created," Sam said, "but your laboratory will be closely monitored. Your need for control could have killed this entire plane and several others. Ariella's lucky she did not carry the mutated strain and your original safeguard worked in reversing her illness. We'll monitor your sickness the best we can and make sure you're comfortable. As long as you are given regular doses of the medication you required Ariella to take, your illness should be manageable."

Linnea let Sam lead her from the room. Dr. Walter looked as if he would beg them to stay, but refrained. As the door closed behind them, she wrapped her arm around her husband's waist as they walked next to the dimly lit crates.

"I can't believe how things have worked out," Linnea said, smiling at her husband. "Though I do feel a little sorry for him, I suppose the punishment is just."

"You have a kind heart, wife." Sam touched her face and then her stomach. His eyes drifted down to her neck where she wore the purple prescription necklace. "I am sorry I haven't been able to cure you."

"And risk our child?" Linnea shook her head. So much had seemed impossible that was now a reality. She was able to have a baby, a husband, a life and a career. "No. Some things are not worth the risk. I can wait. Besides, here, my genetic abnormality doesn't matter."

"There is nothing genetically abnormal about you." He chuckled, trying to kiss her neck. She swatted his arm and forced him to walk out of the old warehouse. He continued, "I am truly a blessed man."

"You are a loved man," she corrected. "I love you, Sam."

"And I you." He stopped just outside the front door as the light streamed onto them and kissed her deeply. Only when she was breathless did he pull his mouth away. "Come, let me take you to our new home. I understand they have a bed."

"A bed?" She laughed. "Just a bed?"

"What else do we need?" With that he swept her up into his arms and whisked her away.

The End

COMPLIMENTARY EXCERPTS

TRY BEFORE YOU BUY!

ABOUT MICHELLE M. PILLOW

New York Times & *USA TODAY*
Bestselling Author

Michelle loves to travel and try new things, whether it's a paranormal investigation of an old Vaudeville Theatre or climbing Mayan temples in Belize. She believes life is an adventure fueled by copious amounts of coffee.

Newly relocated to the American South, Michelle is involved in various film and documentary projects with her talented director husband. She is mom to a fantastic artist. And she's managed by a dog and cat who make sure she's meeting her deadlines.

For the most part she can be found wearing pajama pants and working in her office. There may or may not be dancing. It's all part of the creative process.

Come say hello! Michelle loves talking with readers on social media!

www.MichellePillow.com

facebook.com/AuthorMichellePillow

twitter.com/michellepillow

instagram.com/michellempillow

bookbub.com/authors/michelle-m-pillow

goodreads.com/Michelle_Pillow

amazon.com/author/michellepillow

youtube.com/michellepillow

pinterest.com/michellepillow

LOVE POTIONS

BY MICHELLE M. PILLOW

Warlocks MacGregor® Book 1
Contemporary Paranormal Scottish Warlocks

A little magickal mischief never hurt anyone...

Erik MacGregor, from a clan of ancient Scottish warlocks, isn't looking for love. After centuries, it's not even a consideration...until he moves in next door to Lydia Barratt. It's clear that the shy beauty wants nothing to do with him, but he's drawn to her none-theless and determined to win her over.

Lydia Barratt just wants to be left alone to grow flowers and make lotions in her old Victorian house. The last thing she needs is a demanding Scottish man meddling in her private life. Just because he's gorgeous and totally rocks a kilt doesn't mean she's going to fall for his seductive manner.

But Erik won't give up and just as Lydia let's her guard down, his sister decides to get involved. Her little love potion prank goes terribly wrong, making Lydia the target of his sudden embarrassingly obsessive behavior. They'll have to find a way to pull Erik out of the spell fast when it becomes clear that Lydia has more than a lovesick warlock to worry about. Evil lurks within the shadows and it plans to use Lydia, alive or dead, to take out Erik and his clan for good.

Love Potions Excerpt

"Ly-di-ah! I sit beneath your window, laaaass, singing 'cause I loooove your a—"

"For the love of St. Francis of Assisi, someone call a vet. There is an injured animal screaming in pain outside," Charlotte interrupted the flow of music in ill-humor.

Lydia lifted her forehead from the kitchen table. Her windows and doors were all locked, and yet Erik's endlessly verbose singing penetrated the barrier of glass and wood with ease.

Charlotte held her head and blinked heavily. Her red-rimmed eyes were filled with the all too poignant look of a hangover. She took a seat at the table and laid her head down. Her moan sounded something like, "I'm never moving again."

"You need fluids," Lydia prescribed, getting up to pour unsweetened herbal tea from the pitcher in the fridge. She'd mixed it especially for her friend. It was Gramma Annabelle's hangover recipe of willow bark, peppermint, carrot, and ginger. The old lady always had a fresh supply of it in the house while she was alive. Apparently, being a natural witch also meant in partaking in natural liquors. Annabelle had kept a steady supply of moonshine stashed in the basement. If the concert didn't stop soon she might try to find an old bottle.

"*Ly-di-ah!*"

"Omigod. Kill me," Charlotte moaned. "No. Kill him. Then kill me."

"*Ly-di-ah!*"

Erik had been singing for over an hour. At first, he'd tried to come inside. She'd not invited him and the barrier spell sent him sprawling back into the yard. He didn't seem to mind as he found a seat on some landscaping timbers and began his serenade. The last time she'd asked him to be quiet, he'd gotten louder and overly enthusiastic. In fact, she'd been too scared to pull back the curtains for a clearer look, but she was pretty sure he'd been dancing on her lawn, shaking his kilt.

"Omigod," Charlotte muttered, pushing up and angrily going to a window. Then grimacing, she said, "Is he wearing a tux jacket with his kilt?"

"Don't let him see you," Lydia cried out in a panic. It was too late. The song began with renewed force.

"He's..." Charlotte frowned. "I think it's dancing."

Since the damage was done, Lydia joined Charlotte at the window. Erik grinned. He lifted his arms to the side and kicked his legs, bouncing around the yard like a kid on too much sugar. "Maybe it's a traditional Scottish dance?"

Both women tilted their heads in unison as his kilt kicked up to show his perfectly formed ass.

"He's not wearing..." Charlotte began.

"I know. He doesn't," Lydia answered. Damn, the man had a fine body. Too bad Malina's trick had turned him insane.

To find out more about Michelle's books visit www.MichellePillow.com

FIGHTING LADY JAYNE

THE SERIES CONTINUES

Divinity Warriors Book Two
by Michelle M. Pillow

Alternate Reality Romance

Jayne Hart has earned her independence by becoming Divinity Corporation's inter-dimensional boxing champion. Life is great, until a dirty fighter knocks her unconscious. Now, abandoned by the corporation in a parallel world, Jayne will use every weapon she has to be free once more. Even if it means running from her sexy new "husband" and spending the rest of her life in a primitive forest.

Ronen of Firewall longs for a woman to warm his bed and his home, but he had no intention of choosing a bride. In an unprecedented move, one chooses him. Never in the history of the marriage ceremony has a woman dared to lay claim. How can he resist the alluring Lady Jayne? She's confident and sure in her decision to be with him—until their wedding night when she's nowhere to be found. But, Ronen is not one to shy from a battle. He will find Jayne and, when he does, he has one particular "weapon" in mind for taming his seductive, wayward wife.

Extended Prologue Excerpt

Getting her teeth knocked around in her head hurt like hell, but being able to spit blood into the face of her opponent more than made up for the discomfort. Jayne "The Sweet" Hart laughed as Big Bobby Bishop sputtered in anger. She knew he expected her to cry at the landed blow. Truth was, part of Jayne did want to cry. She wasn't a glutton for a beating, and that last hit had left blood running out of her mouth at a steady flow. They'd been going at it for nearly a half hour, bare-knuckle boxing—no protective gear beyond any sanctioned bioengineering, no referees, not like some of the other dimensions had. No, here on dimensional plane 241 almost anything was legal. That's why the gladiator ring paid such big money and drew the notice of rich, inter-dimensional travelers who could afford a private plane jump through Divinity Corporation. It's also why Jayne agreed to travel from her own world to this alternate reality where laws were more of a suggestion and killing someone in a fight was considered a good thing.

In many ways, each alternate reality was like drifting through time on her own home plane, had a singular event on the timeline been changed. Each dimension seemed to be a different outcome to a similar historical start. Some were so technologically advanced everything was done for them, and they'd found a worldwide peace and understanding. Jayne generally stayed away from those levels of existence. There wasn't much employment for fighters in such realities.

Other planes hadn't even developed a means of fast communication beyond throwing a bird into the air with a tiny letter tied to its leg. Still others had just installed their first aqueducts or invented their first vehicles to run without horses or oxen. Or, like 241, they had every technological comfort and yet somehow managed to maintain their barbarian sensibilities.

Any way you looked at it, Earth was Earth, just different versions of itself—same languages, matching natural events, some people looked the same but weren't. Humans, for the most part, still resembled humans. And those with power were still greedy bastards trying to tell her how to do her job.

Big Bobby watched her expectantly, his mouth opened as if to scream in victory at any second. Jayne knew he expected her to fall with that punch. She watched as the excitement slowly died from his eyes, replaced by shock, then confusion, until finally a boiling rage. His eyes scanned the crowd before moving toward the large balcony to where his daddy sat watching. Big Bobby's father and known gangster boss had undoubtedly assured his halfwit-of-a-lug-nut son that he was a sure winner. It wouldn't have been so bad if Big Bobby had been an admirable opponent, but after a half hour, she could still see out of one of her eyes, and he only managed to knock her off her feet twice.

And Bossman Bishop wanted her to take a dive to this chump?

Jayne snorted. Not bloody likely. She'd never work as a boxer again—not that she had to. In her home dimension, she had plenty of money to bide her twelve lifetimes.

Divinity Corp paid her big for this fight. They were her ticket home and had the only known source of inter-dimensional travel technology on this plane. Natural slips were extremely rare and the timing of them completely predictable by the company, even if they didn't know where the slip would go. If they didn't take her home, she'd be stuck until the end of time. Besides, there was no way she was taking a dive just because the local gangsters had promised to...

What had Bossman said again? Oh, yeah. They were going to gang rape her grandma while she watched. It had hardly been a threat. Jayne was an orphan. Still, a part of her was up in arms for the hypothetical grandmother they'd threatened.

There was no way Bossman could know about her lack of family. The publicity put out by Divinity Corp's entertainment division fostered the wholesome image of their Sweetheart Jayne. Of course, it was all a lie. They hired a family to take pictures with her at a rented country home—the devoted mother, the fake twin sister with a poor health condition, the baby brother and suit 'n' cravat dad.

The loud, almost fanatical cheering of the crowd grew. They surrounded on all sides, lining the rows upon rows of rotating theater seats. Every few minutes, the seats would shift, changing the angle from which a person watched. Lights flashed all around her. Floating cameras zipped by her head, but she ignored them. Most of the bets were on her and she never lost a fight. Never. And she would be damned if she gave this guy the reputation of being the one person who could take her down. He didn't deserve the title or her respect. Rage grew within her that he even dared to presume he was worthy of taking her down.

Do it for your family, Jayne, she thought sardonically.

Jayne decided to teach him and Bossman a lesson. She drew her body around, preparing to kick him upside the head in a move she knew he wouldn't see coming. Big Bobby swung again. She dodged the blow, and this time his hand merely grazed her cheek, stinging the cut she had there. She didn't hesitate. Whipping her leg around, she swung it for his head. Suddenly, every nerve in her body exploded with pain. There was no stopping her body's momentum as it lifted off the hard mat. The noise of the crowd faded and grew until stopping altogether. Big Bobby caught her suddenly slowed foot and pushed her backward. Nothing was as it should be. Lights streaked in her vision before her body was abruptly stopped by a metal pole slamming into her back. Then, darkness clouded her mind and she could only think one thing.

Boxers' Poison.

For a complete, up-to-date booklist, visit www. MichellePillow.com

PLEASE LEAVE A REVIEW

THANK YOU FOR READING!

Please take a moment to share your thoughts by reviewing this book.

Be sure to check out Michelle's other titles at

www.michellepillow.com

www.ingramcontent.com/pod-product-compliance
Lightning Source LLC
Chambersburg PA
CBHW030634120726
47904CB00006B/2147